MY LOVE
MY HEART

The Reunion

Euphemia Chukwu

Published by
Fame Star Media

Unit 7, Studio Court
28 Lawrence Road
South Tottenham
London
N15 4ER

+447446234704
Website: www.famestaragency.com
Email: info@famestaragency.com

ISBN: 978-0-9957695-1-9

For more copies, feedback or questions, you can contact the author on:

www.facebook.com/euphemia.chu
www.facebook.com/Theladyfame
www.twitter.com/euphemiachukwu
www.linkedin.com/in/euphemia-chukwu
www.instagram.com/meuphemia

Chapter One

The Big Reveal

On the drive back home after leaving Anthony's, the whole incident in Mandy's room at the hospital played back in my mind.

"Alright.... enough with the pleasantries," Mandy whined, "What's this I hear about your engagement? Not only that, I heard it from the news report," waving the newspaper at us.

Shocked by her comments, I walked over to her and snatched the paper from her to see; forgetting she was still fragile. I saw a picture of Gianni and me on the front page. I read the headline and a bit more but I didn't believe what I read. I flopped down on the chair with my mouth wide opened.

"I can't believe that your Gianni Canuti is 'The Gianni Canuti;' the only son of 'The Canuti Family,' one of the richest Italian mafia families in the world," Mandy blurted out in excitement. "My best friend and his fiancé are engaged.. Wow! That's exciting!" She added.

I looked up at Gianni as he bit his lower lip and looked at me with concern. I glanced back at the newspaper still in disbelief. I looked at Mandy who was happy about the news. She stood up slowly, and walked towards the door dumbstruck by the revelation.

"What, she didn't know?" I heard Mandy asking.

"No," replied Gianni in a somber tone as he followed me out.

Once we were in the car, he started explaining but I told him to just take me home. We were both silent as we traveled back home. When we got to my house, I opened the car to get out; almost immediately, he called my name. I pause but could not look at him. "I love you," he said, with insecurity in his voice.

Ignoring him, I got out and closed the car door not looking back. Once I got in, I shut the door and pressed my back against it.

Moments later, I took off my shoes and jacket, dropped my handbag on the chair and went straight to pour a stiff drink of cognac for me. I clenched my teeth and shut my eyes tightly feeling the burning sensation down my throat and chest. Once the burning stopped, I poured another; this time, sitting down on the chair and swinging it back and forth. I turned on the T.V flicking through the channels until one station caught my eyes. I turned up the volume — the news was about Gianni Canuti's engagement, the only grandson of the mafia boss, Luciano Canuti.

I went and poured more drink for myself. I flopped down on my sofa and stared up at the ceiling. I shut my eyes and remembered all that had transpired the past two days when I had no idea who Gianni was. His mom and dad seemed so nice; how did I miss that? Suddenly, everything began to make sense; each time we went to restaurants or hotels anywhere, they treated him in a most deferential manner. Come to think of it; his mom's name, Rosa, must be the name they had given the hotel, Rosa, in New York where we stayed. I started to tremble as the memories flooded my mind.

Unsure how to feel, I got up to get another shot of cognac. My hand was shaking as I held the glass; images of our last night in

New York was plaguing my mind. Why did he lie to me? How could he look me in the eye and lie all those years? I knocked back my drink, grabbed my handbag, got my shoes on, and stormed out to go and confront him. I struggled to open the door to my car with the key dropping to the ground as my hand was quivering. I supported myself by leaning against the car then I began to cry. From nowhere, I felt someone behind me. I turned around quickly almost jumpy. It was Gianni. He picked up my car keys and held it out to me looking remorseful.

"You had no right to keep this from me," I said sobbing, angry and hurt.

"I'm sorry," he apologized and moved close to comfort me. I pulled back, still angry.

"You lied to me," I said with tears in my eyes.

"I'm really sorry," he repeated repentantly.

Choked up with my tears, I couldn't speak out "Wh……why?" I croaked.

Before he could answer, I put my hand up to stop him. "You know what? I thought I could do this but I can't; I can't do this. I need some space; I need to be on my own; I need to think," I said with tears streaming down my cheeks.

I took my car keys from his hand and went back inside.

I tried to stop the flashbacks and get the revelation of the true identity of my fiancé out of my mind lest I start crying again. I was so deep in thought that I did not realize when I got home. The first thing I saw was Gianni's car parked outside — that was the last thing I needed. Reluctantly, I got out of my car and closed the door wondering where he was as I could not see him in the car. Then I felt his presence behind me as he spoke, "So now you are going to dump me and get back with him, huh?" Still with my back to him, I lowered my head in exasperation. He grabbed my arm roughly and swang me around to face him.

"Let go of me," I said, snatching my arm back angrily.

His face was unshaven and rough as he stared at me with jealousy written all over his face. "Have you been following me around or have you had me followed? After all, isn't that what you mafias do?" I snorted at him but he ignored my comment.

"Do you still love him?" He asked bitterly.

"Yes I do and I always will," I replied.

"I will kill him," he said storming off.

I ran in front of him stopping him in his tracks, "The real you is coming out now, isn't it?" I yelled.

"I forgot that that's what you mafia people do when you don't like someone; you bump them off. If you lay a finger on him I will never forgive you or ever talk to you again."

"He's Mr. Safe, isn't he? Mr. Perfect; howbeit, if he is so perfect, why do you always run off with other guys only to get back together with him, huh? Is that how you get your kicks? You know what, maybe the newspapers were right when they said you should do fellows out there a favor and just marry Anthony instead of breaking men's hearts. You give them false hope only to go running back to him," he said, shouting at me.

"Yeah! Well, maybe I should," I yelled back at him.

I was puzzled at his comment. The newspaper report was years ago when I was still in university; I wondered how he knew of it. Right there and then, I knew I needed some space. As I turned to leave, he looked so sad, almost afraid. He ran in front of me.

"I'm sorry, I…I am afraid that if I leave you alone I may lose you," he pleaded.

"If you don't leave me alone, you will lose me," I said sternly. "Do you know why Anthony and I have lasted as long as we have and still remain close friends?"

"So I should let you sleep with other guys like Anthony," he said childishly and disrespectfully.

"I can't talk to you when you're like this. You know what; at least with him, I know where I stand. I know he loves me; good or bad he is always there. He is dependable and most importantly, he is honest," I defended.

He put his hand to my left cheek looking into my eyes, "I love you, Cara," he said tenderly.

"Please don't do this," I pleaded weakly hating myself for wanting to kiss him badly.

"Ti amo, Tesoro – I love you, my darling," he said almost in a whisper as he leaned over and kissed me lovingly. The kiss became more passionate. I hated myself for being weak. My whole body yearned for his touch.

What was it about him that made me lose control whenever I was with him? I never knew. I felt so drawn to him even though I was still angry with him. I pulled away from him with my right hand on his chest.

"A lot has happened the last few days and I need time to process everything; I know it's hard but you have to let me be. I am going on a holiday to be on my own; I will be away from everyone and everything. I will be back before the ball. I will leave first thing tomorrow," I said and started to walk away leaving him there helpless; then I went back and kissed him gently. "Ti amo," I whispered as he stood there watching me walk away.

Throughout the night, I could not sleep. Everything in my life was so unsettled that I felt empty and alone. One minute I had everything, the next I had nothing. Was this God's way of getting my attention? I felt so confused and unsure about everything. Here I was; I couldn't imagine my life without Anthony but it felt right whenever I was with Gianni. I was tired of thinking too much. I picked up the phone to call Anthony as he was always the one to talk to whenever I felt so low but I put the phone down realizing I had to learn to live without him. I dialed Gianni's number and cut it but he called back. "You can't sleep too, huh?" He asked.

I did not reply. He then asked if he could come but I declined since it wouldn't solve anything. I said good night and put the phone down. I went to get a glass of water only for my phone to ring again; I thought it was Gianni.

"Darling, please I need to be left alone. I'm sorry for calling you," I said emotionally drained.

"Sorry, dear; it's Rosa, Gianni's mother. I got your number from my son. I hope you don't mind?" she asked.

"No, of course not. Sorry about the mix up. I thought it was Gianni calling back again," I said sitting up and very surprised to hear from her.

She apologized for the way I found out about Gianni's identity. She also apologized on behalf of her son for lying to me.

"You see, dear, my son has loved you for a great many years even before you started going out; and when the Canuti men love, they love with great passion; they don't hold back," she added. I started to cry.

"Oh my beautiful daughter, don't cry. Everything will be fine; nothing worth having ever comes easy and I can honestly tell you my son is worth it. Please find it in your heart to forgive him," she pleaded.

We spoke for a while longer. I felt better speaking with her. She prayed with me and said she looked forward to seeing me at the family house soon. I told her I was going away for a few days to clear my head. She understood and added that I should take as long as I needed.

In the morning, I woke up early, had breakfast, got showered and called my ex-foster mom, Mrs. Abbott. I had a sudden urge to pay her a visit. After our conversation, I packed few clothes in my hand luggage and left. I drove around for hours just thinking about my life and how far I had come.

Chapter Two

A Trip to My Past

I drove past my old school and the group home. I took a turn onto the road leading to Mrs. Abbott's. When I got there, I parked my car outside of the house. For a moment, I wondered whether or not to go in. After a bit of contemplation, I decided that since I was going down the memory lane, it would not be complete without stopping there, too. I got out of my car and rang the doorbell. Mrs. Abbott opened the door with a look of surprise and a glitter of happiness to see me.

"Sandra! What a surprise to see you here! Is everything alright? I thought you would be busy planning the wedding of the year," she said, obviously pleased with the news of my engagement.

"So you have heard then," I said walking inside.

She looked at me puzzled and closed the door behind her. She followed me to the sitting room. I looked around the house;

nothing much had changed since I left years ago.

"So is Mr. Abbott still in jail?" I asked picking up the photo frame of the two of them by the cabinet table. They looked so happy and in love. Mr. Abbott was gazing at her with his piercing blue eyes with her looking lovingly at him with her big brown eyes. They looked like a perfect couple. She walked over and took the photo from me and put it back faced down. She started rubbing her hands frantically.

"I should have gotten rid of that years ago," she said, "I think he should be out but I really don't care. He is not my problem anymore; after all, we are divorced."

"And how do you feel about that since you are now a born-again Christian?" I asked her, curious.

"I wish I knew what I know now; I married him while young. I thought I knew him; I thought he loved me but there is only one true love and that is the love of Jesus Christ. Don't get me wrong; I am sure your fiancé, Gianni, loves you." She looked at me in a curious manner and continued, "I must admit it was quite a surprise that you were not getting married to Anthony after all these years you've been together; his parents are so disappointed — they already call me in-law," she said laughing.

"I know you have these two men who love you very much and would do anything for you but I don't want you to rely solely on their love. You need the love of God; the agape love. Only God can give you this unconditional love because the love of man will always disappoint but that of God never disappoints. I don't want you to pin all your hopes and love on a person only for them to disappoint you," she said looking down sullenly for a moment.

"You have gone through so much already. I know if not for God, you would not pull through. Please think about it and give your life to Christ. He loves you and He is knocking at the door of your heart and waiting," she continued; rubbing my left arm.

I sat down there on the old sofa deep in thoughts and processing everything she had related to me. Mrs. Abbott suddenly got up.

"Oh! I have something of yours; wait here," she said and left the room.

I wondered for a moment what it could be — I thought I took everything when I moved out. She came back with a framed picture and handed it over to me.

"You used to paint her quite a lot when you were younger; I thought you might want to keep it. I framed it for you. She is so beautiful and I often wondered if she was someone important from your past."

"Yes, she was," I said staring at the painting.

"She was my mother! I used to see her a lot when I was younger; she helped me get through difficult times over the years. She and my dad died when I was two years old — they were murdered," I said casually, not really wanting to get into it. She came closer and gave me a hug.

"Sweetheart, I am so sorry; what a horrible thing to live with! I am surprised you have kept yourself well-disciplined all these years and not only that, you have turned out to be such a wonderful young lady. I am so proud of you," she said with a look of joy.

After giving me another hug, she went and made us something to eat. After dinner, I narrated to her everything that had happened: from Gianni's proposal in New York to coming home to the news of Mandy beaten up by her boyfriend and her ending up in the hospital, to finding out Gianni's true identity and then finally finding Anthony and Joanne in bed together. She was so shocked by all the revelations that she poured us a large glass of rum. We both drank in silence as we soaked in everything. When my glass was empty, she poured me some more.

"I thought born-again believers don't drink," I said jokingly.

"The Bible does not condemn drinking alcohol; what it condemns is overdoing it and getting drunk," she said pouring another one for herself as we both laughed.

We had such a relaxing time. I was happy I paid her a visit; it felt so good. I requested to stay the night and didn't mind when she suggested I sleep in my old room. Later on when I went up to sleep, it was strange at first but I eventually fell asleep. In the morning, I woke up and went downstairs only to see that Mrs. Abbott was all dressed up. Breakfast was made and on the table just like how it used to be when I first joined the family years back. Funny enough, I was famished; I ate until I was filled. I looked up at Mrs. Abbott who was always a slow eater still eating. I thought about how she always looked pretty with her curly hair although one could see traces of gray in her black hair; probably from stress because she was not that old.

Just then, it dawned on me that her birthday was coming up soon and I knew exactly what to do for her. She must have felt me staring because she looked up, I smiled and excused myself to go and get ready. I decided to give her an early birthday present. When I got back to my room, I made a call to book a luxury holiday cottage in the stunning Cartmel Valley in the South Lake District area of Cumbria. When I was done showering, I came down to tell her the good news. There was a spark in her eyes. She was so delighted that she ran upstairs to her room like a child to pack. We left by midday as it was about five hours' drive. We arrived in the evening. The cottage was furnished and equipped to a very high standard and immaculately presented. We checked into our room. I dropped my bag and went straight to soak in the bath.

"You and Gianni made the news again," she said as I came out of the bathroom.

"Oh Great! I came here to get away from all that and now I can't go out," I said flopping down on the chair in my robe with the towel on my hair.

"I wanted us to go out to have dinner; the village pubs serve first-class food," I said sulking.

"Don't let that spoil your holiday. We can still go out," she said.

"Just don't think about anything. Come on, let me help you blow dry your hair then get ready; I'm hungry."

We walked to the village pub. It was quite busy when we got there so I slipped in quietly and sat down in the corner while Mrs. Abbott went to place our order. I kept the menu held high covering my face until she came back with our drinks. Not long after, the waitress came over and took our order for the food; it was delicious.

The strangest thing occurred after our meal when I asked for the bill. The waitress said that the manager wanted to speak to me if I didn't mind. Suspecting that there might be a problem, I told her that I did mind and demanded my bill. Just then, the manager came over holding a black LG mobile phone in his hand and a small pad with a pen. As I looked at them wondering what was going on, the barman came over with a bottle of champagne and two glasses. The manager looked at me smiling as if star-struck.

"Sorry to disturb your dinner, Miss Appleton," he said, "Please accept this bottle of champagne from the pub congratulating you on your engagement and don't worry about the bill; it's on the house as an appreciation for choosing to dine in our establishment; we are really honored. Did you enjoy the food?"

"Yes, we did," I said looking at Mrs. Abbott who was fascinated by all that was happening.

"Can I have your autograph, please, if it's not too much trouble? It's for my nephew, you know; he's got all the magazines of you and posters in his room. Is it alright if I took a picture with you to prove to him that you were really here?" He asked excitedly.

"Sure," I said standing up.

He quickly gave his mobile phone to the waiter to take the picture. He moved closer as he posed for the camera. He thanked me and left. Mrs. Abbott squealed in delight.

"So is this what it is like to be a celebrity?" she asked smiling.

Just when I thought I had gotten away, some more people came over for autographs. So I rushed my drink and left the pub before a reporter turned up. When we got back to the cottage, I was shattered. I just crushed on top of my bed in my clothes and fell asleep.

When I woke up, I saw a missed call from Gianni and a text from Mandy. Before I could reply anyone, Mrs. Abbott knocked on the door and came in with a brand new hiking boots in her hands.

"Come on chop, chop, you don't have time for that," she said taking the phone from me and hurrying me out of bed.

"I have been waiting for you to wake up. We are already late so go hop in the shower. We will grab something to eat on the way."

"On the way to what? Where are we going?" I asked looking puzzled as I climbed out of bed.

"Hiking, of course," she said holding up the boots and smiling.

"These are for you. I went out to buy them in the local shops while you were asleep. They have beautiful sights here; you would love them. I know you would like to paint the beautiful picturesque view of the countryside so I bought you these brushes and paint plus paper. You are going to love it," she said enthusiastically.

I showered quickly and wore something casual with my hiking boots. I grabbed my phone and car keys to go but Mrs. Abbott wagged her finger and said no phones or cars and that we were walking. I didn't bother to protest as I knew it would be of no use. We stopped at a café to have breakfast. She ordered full English breakfast for both of us saying we needed the energy for the hike. We bought some food and drinks for the picnic. After eating, we got up and set off for our hiking. She showed me some beautiful sights. I know she must have been there before because she seemed so at ease. She really loved nature walks while I was more of the sand, sea and cocktail kind of person. We must have been walking for hours as my legs were really hurting. I wanted to stop but she insisted it was just a little further even though she had been saying that for two hours. She promised we were nearly there and assured me it was only ten minutes away. I mustered every ounce of energy I had and continued. After thirty more minutes, my legs could no longer carry me any further. I sat down on the grass and refused to move.

"I suppose this is a good spot for a picnic," she said, setting down her rucksack. She looked around appreciating nature. I had not seen her relaxed and alive like that before. I looked around and the view, indeed, was breathtakingly beautiful. Although hiking was not my thing, I could not help but admire and appreciate such beauty. I knew I had to capture it in my painting so after our picnic, I began to paint. I did two separate paintings; one was the natural view and the other was a portrait of Mrs. Abbott. She was so moved and happy that a tear came down her cheeks.

On looking at her watch, she asked for us to get back before it got dark. We packed up and trekked back. By the time we got to our cottage, it was dark. I was so tired that after taking a quick shower, I went to bed. When I woke up in the morning, Mrs. Abbott had packed all her things waiting anxiously for me. She had to get back to London immediately. She explained that something had come up at her workplace that needed her urgent attention.

I got ready as quickly as I could and we headed home. When we arrived at her residence, she insisted that I came in to eat something since I had not eaten since morning. I rushed off to bath while she made food for us. After my bath, food was ready. It was a nice meal of chicken and rice with potato salad.

I stayed with her until about 7 pm before I left. I got home very exhausted. I sat on the bed and decided to cool off a bit only to realize I was fast asleep.

I did not wake up until midday. I couldn't believe I hadn't spoken to or seen Gianni, Anthony, Mandy or anyone of them in days. I really missed Gianni very much. I wanted to see him and hold him so bad. I picked up the phone and called to know if he could come around and within 30 minutes, he was at mine. Without any dressing or making up, I wanted him to see me plain with my hair messed up. He had lost a bit of weight and had a serious look on. I guess I should have given him a kiss when I opened the door. He too was unsure what to do so he waited for me to make the first move but I was a bit nervous so I walked back to my bedroom. He closed the front door and followed me to the room without saying a word.

"Do you care for a drink?" I asked.

"Would I need it?" He asked with a taut smile.

I smiled back sitting on my bed. I stretched out my hand to him and he came and sat next to me. His eyes were filled with love and trepidation. I stroked his left cheek and he took my hand and kissed my palm.

"I have missed you so much," I said and he gave a deep sigh of relief.

"I thought you were going to leave me," he said.

I gave him a hug and kissed his neck.

"I could never leave you; I love you far too much," I whispered.

He held me tighter like a child who was secure in their mother's loving arms. I ran my fingers through his soft dark hair gently and we stayed like that for a while; happy to be back in each other's arms.

"I'm sorry; it's the biggest mistake I have ever made," he said, "I promise I will never…,"

"Shhh! I know you didn't mean to hurt me and I understand why you did it but none of it matters now. All that matter is our love for each other and where we go from here."

He pulled away from me suddenly and jumped off the bed and got on one knee pulling out my engagement ring from his pocket.

"Well, in that case, will you marry me, Sandra?" He asked. I giggled and shifted to the edge of the bed.

"Before I could answer that, I think there are few things you need to know about me," I said.

"I know all I need to know about you.... and that is you are the woman I want to spend the rest of my life with and I can't imagine my life without you. I love you so much, Cara. I have been in love with you for a very, very long time and I will still love you until I die," he said sincerely as he held my left hand and gazed up into my eyes. "You always know what to say and, of course, I will marry you. I love you, Gianni, and I always will," I replied.

He slipped the ring on my finger and he got up and kissed me passionately on the lips. I laid back on the bed with him on top of me. The kiss became more and more erotic as he pushed my legs open with his body, moving his kisses slowly down to my breasts. I groaned with excitement and whispered weakly, "Don't you think we should wait....mmm, until after the wedding?"

"Yeah, mmm… after this one," he replied taking off my robes, and unhooking my bra while taking off my G-string.

I kissed his neck raising my body closer to his. Our bodies yearned so much for each other's touch; we couldn't stop even if we wanted to; the passion was so strong we yielded to it. I unbuttoned his shirt and took it off then I unbuckled his belt taking off his trousers then his pants. We made love again and again until we could no longer move. We lay in each other's arms, blissfully happy and satisfied. We did not go anywhere or do anything the whole weekend other than making love, eat, shower and make love again. We were in our own private world where it was just the two of us. We could run around naked without a care in the world.

Later in the day, my house phone rang and the machine picked it up and it was Rosa.

"Sandra, Gianni; I know you are there and I am very happy you have worked things out but I do need to speak with both of you. Since you are not picking your mobile phones, I decided to call the house phone but if you don't pick up, I will just have to come over there," she said.

15

Gianni leaped out of bed and quickly picked up the handset, "Mama!" He said almost breathless.

"I knew you would see sense. I take it Sandra can hear me; I want both of you to come to dinner in the evening; I want to spend some time with my daughter-in-law and this time, no rushing off to work. We are at the main house in Surrey so we shall see you both later. Make sure you pack some clothes to wear, Sandra; be good children," she said blowing a kiss on the phone to us. Gianni put the phone down and we laughed and rolled back to bed.

The house in Surrey was about twenty-nine miles' drive. It was their main home for relaxation. After spending some more time in each other's arms, we got changed and set off. Realizing we would be late, Gianni rang his mom and assured her we were on our way. We exchanged love gazes from time to time and kissed. Intermittently, I would rub his thighs.

"Oh! I don't think you want to do that if you want us to get to the house in one piece." He gave me a quick glance then kept his eyes back on the road. When we finally arrived, I gazed at the mansion in awe. Gianni smiled and began to tell me about the house.

"The property is approached through large ornamental wrought iron gates mounted on high stone piers with further piers and splays on each side. The drive descends towards the house and is guarded by low brick walls. It then splits into three directions; to the right, it descends to the underground parking; to the center, it widens under the port-cochère into a large turning area with marble paving; the third continues round to the staff and guest accommodation; it also has a manager's area and secondary garaging," he narrated.

"Wow!" I exclaimed as the iron gates opened. He drove in and continued, "We have about twenty bedrooms and just about the same bathrooms plus fifteen reception rooms. My dad and I love cars so there is underground garaging for at least eight cars and a helipad for private landings. My mom loves to entertain a lot so the main house has been organized on a scale to allow for ambassadorial entertainment as well as a conventional private family living. On the ground floor, there is a triple height reception area with marble flooring and French doors leading on to an extensive terrace overlooking the gardens. The ground floor, surrounded by wide marble terraces providing access to the gardens, incorporates a grand hallway, a sunken reception area, as well as bar and dining areas. The east wing holds the master bedroom suite consisting of a sitting area, bedroom and bathroom, a limed oak corridor between the bedroom and the bathroom, direct access to the east wing pool balcony and the glass lift to the pool area.

There are two powder rooms, a conference room, and a library/reading room; that one is for mom and dad. The west wing at ground floor level includes a cherry-paneled office, open plan breakfast room and kitchen, private sitting room, two further powder rooms and the banqueting hall. There is also access to the west wing pool which is designed on a Roman theme with marble pillars. It provides a beauty salon, sauna and male and female dressing rooms. The first floor incorporates eight bedroom/bathroom suites. Each is individually designed with balcony access. The penthouse floor is mine and I am sure you will stay in the other suite because it's divided into two suites; each comprising of two bedrooms, a bathroom, a shower room and a powder room, dressing room and a walkthrough sitting/dining room.

There is a terrace with infinity pool and central leisure/reception area. There are also three balconies/terraces, including the large terrace over the port-cochère. The basement of the property includes an underground garage which can hold up to eight cars like I said. There are various store rooms and the industrial kitchen with areas reserved for cold rooms, freezer rooms, and a washroom. There's a corridor leading from the garage which accesses a glass lobby and leads into the bowling alley and the gymnasium area. Close by are the male and female changing rooms, the cinema and the wine cellar. There is also a walk-in strong room/safe, a billiard/snooker area and a squash court. The principal lift has been designed to service all floors and there is a separate lift to connect the industrial kitchen with the breakfast room.

I hope you like horses because we have a huge stable and mom loves to ride and would insist you go riding with her. Attached to the three-bedroom guest accommodation building is the block providing further garaging for four vehicles, the laundry and the estate manager's office with en suite facilities.

The gatehouse incorporates two bedrooms, a conservatory, a kitchen/breakfast room, a sitting room, two separate powder rooms, a security room and a waiting area. There are also two pool houses on the estate; one by each of the outside pools. There are two separate guest properties. One consists of six bedrooms with en suite bathrooms, a kitchen/dining area, and an upstairs sitting room. The other includes three bedrooms with en suite bathrooms, a kitchen/dining area, and upstairs sitting room and that just about covers it," he said complacently.

"How many swimming pools?" I asked surprised at the grandness of the mansion.

"There are about four pools and the Jacuzzi which you will love. I can't wait for us to try it out," he said leaning over to kiss me.

"Mmm, after the wedding," I said, pushing his lips away with my finger.

His mom and dad came out of the house as they saw our car pull up. They were followed by the attendants.

"Welcome back, sir and Miss Sandra," the older attendant greeted whilst the younger one just smiled and went to get our luggage from the car.

Rosa and Giovanni approached us with smiles. After hugging, kissing, and exchanging pleasantries, Rosa and I linked arms and walked towards the house while Gianni and his dad walked behind us. I couldn't get over how beautiful the house was as I looked around.

"You have a magnificent house," I said to her.

"Oh! If you think so wait until you see the family house in Italy," she said smiling.

"Would you like a tour of the estate?" She asked.

"Oh! Yes, please!" I said in excitement.

"Gianni can show you the house briefly but you can have a proper tour tomorrow as it is late now. Gianni will show you your room then we can have dinner," she said patting my hand.

Gianni and I walked up the spiral staircase as I gazed up at the huge golden crystal chandeliers. Mr. and Mrs. Canuti walked up the other side. I thought to myself, "This place must have cost at least a billion pounds or something." I have never seen anything like it. No wonder Gina fought tooth and nail to hold on to Gianni. I wondered for a moment if she had been to this house; interrupting my thoughts, "This is your room," said Gianni. "Wow!" I said looking around.

My luggage was already there. He took me to his suite then he showed me the whole floor. After, he accompanied me back to my suite. He suggested that we should shower and get ready for dinner as we were late. I sat on the big king-size bed stroking it sensually and motioned him with my index finger to join me.

"This bed would be awfully lonely tonight without you in it with me," I said.

"So will mine," he replied.

"Have I told you how much I love?" I asked gazing into his eyes.

"I have this feeling like.....me being here, being with you is so right. I feel so at home, you know....like a sense of belonging. I love you so much and I love your mom and dad even though I have not known them for long; I just feel like I have known them all my life," I said.

"You do belong here and yes, my parents love you almost as much as I love you especially my mom," he said holding my hand.

I gave him a hug then he left to go and get changed.

By the time I was done showering and came downstairs, Gianni was already there. One of the maids met me at the base of the stairs and took me to the dining room where everyone was seated at the dinner table. It was beautifully laid out with beautiful Chinese plates. I sat opposite Gianni and apologized for keeping them waiting. Without delay, the maids served the food. It was splendid.

We went to the private sitting room after dinner where they had a huge collection of admirable paintings.

"Do you like paintings?" Giovanni asked.

I nodded my head and said yes. He told me stories about each painting. There was a beautiful family portrait of them there. They looked like such a happy family; which they were. I moved from one family portrait to the other when my eyes caught a photo of two handsome men holding each other on the shoulder in a pose. One looked like Gianni, the other was a mixed race black guy with a beautiful smile and dark brown eyes. Giovanni noticed I was staring at the photo and came over.

"That was me in my younger days with my best friend, Angelo. We were much younger than you and my son when that was taken," he said remorsefully.

Gianni and his mom came closer. "You look so much like your dad; very handsome," I said to Gianni.

"Thank you very much, Cara," Giovanni said, with his face brightening up.

"Yes, the Canuti men are very handsome," Rosa said. We both smiled in agreement then she continued, "It is getting late, though, and we have a lot to discuss. Let's have an early night as we will wake up early in the morning to go horse riding."

I looked over at Gianni and raised an eyebrow. Rosa noticed my apprehension and reassured me that it wouldn't be difficult to learn after I told her that never once had I ever ridden a horse. She kissed Gianni and me goodnight and so did Giovanni; then they left us alone.

"Don't stay up too long, children," Rosa cautioned. Gianni and I sat by the fireplace and held each other in silence not wanting to part to our separate rooms. After a while, we got up and said our goodnights and headed off to our suite.

Chapter Three

Alexis Santiago

"Aahh!" I screamed as the black stallion galloped faster and faster. I held on for my dear life and was certain my heart must have been thumping a thousand beats a second. The horse came to a stop where Giovanni and Rosa were as they climbed down. Gianni rode over to my side and stopped. I held on to the horse firmly and afraid to let go. He laughed and got down from his horse to help me get off the horse. I held on to him so tight that I didn't want him to put me down. Rosa came over to us and asked if I was okay.

"Oh yes, everything is fine" I said slightly embarrassed. They all smiled as I tried to hide the pain I felt.

"Good, let's head back. Breakfast should be ready soon," said Rosa.

"Head back...you mean back on the horse? Can't we just walk

back?" I asked almost pleading.

"It is too far to walk but we would take it easy this time, I promise," said Rosa reassuring.

When we got back to the house, I could hardly walk. My whole body hurt. I could not quite work out which part of horse riding I was supposed to love as Rosa said earlier. While the groom took my horse, I waddled behind Gianni's parents as Gianni caught up with me after handing his horse over. He asked if I was okay while laughing at the way I was walking. His parents turned around and joined him laughing. Notwithstanding I was in so much agony, I couldn't help but laugh with them. When I got to my room, I threw off the riding outfit and went to run a hot bath bubbling with the sweet smell of sea salts and aloe vera. I was so relaxed in the bath that I must have stayed longer than I should. Gianni came over and stood there for a little while watching; I pretended not to notice.

"Do you want to come in and join me? I asked teasingly.

"Don't tempt me," he said bringing the white towel as I climbed out of the bath. He wrapped it around me lovingly.

"I take it you are feeling much better?" he asked.

"Yes, I feel much, much better but I should hurry, right? I'm late for breakfast, I know," I said feeling bad.

"Don't worry, they understand. In fact, tu il mio tesoro sei una stella - you, my darling, are a star. You did really well for your first time," he said.

"Now you are humoring me," I said smiling as I got dressed.

"No, really, you did well. I'm not just saying that but my parents were even impressed," he said sincerely as he helped me with my zipper. I brushed my hair and we went down for breakfast.

After breakfast, Gianni and his dad went out while Rosa gave me a tour of the whole estate. It was even bigger than Gianni described. She introduced me to the workers and her horses.

"This black Arabian stallion is Sebastian; it's yours," she said as she handed it over to me.

I didn't know what to say as I was still afraid of the big horse; but it was beautiful. Sensing my fear, she said, "You don't have to be scared. He won't hurt you....here."

She handed me a packet of apple snacks for horses and asked me to feed him. I poured some into my palm and hesitantly moved my hand towards his mouth. As Sebastian moved closer to eat the snacks, I shut one eye while watching anxiously with the other. It ate the snacks from my hand and seemed to enjoy it. I became more comfortable and moved closer and rubbed him slowly.

"You like that, huh? You are a good boy; aren't you? Yes, you are. We are going to be such good friends," I said to the horse.

Rosa left the two of us alone. We were well acquainted when she got back. The groom came back and took Sebastian to the stables. We went back to the house and had a light lunch talking about the wedding and the engagement. The more I got to know Gianni's mom, the more I liked her. She was so loving that I couldn't believe how well we got along. Gianni and his dad were not yet back; Rosa had some calls to make so I went up to the roof terrace as it was such a lovely sunny day. One of the maids brought me a glass of red wine. I asked him for a paper and pen or paint and brush if there were any around. Fifteen minutes later, he came back with a brand new paint, brush, and paper.

I painted the wonderful woodland and for some reason, I felt like painting my mom standing next to Sebastian. Just as I finished painting, Rosa came up to join me.

"I didn't know you could paint? You are really good."

She picked up the one with my mom and Sebastian. She looked intently at the painting and her face went pale. I enquired if she was alright; she quickly asked where and how I knew the lady in the painting. Gianni and his dad joined us before I could reply. I got up and ran toward him giving him a kiss and a hug. Giovanni kissed Rosa on the lips warmly as he sat next to her.

Rosa covered up my painting and suggested we head back down to the sitting room as time for dinner was near. I picked up my paper with the paintings inside. Gianni and I walked ahead hand in hand with his parents behind us. We chatted happily as I filled him in on everything that happened while they were away. When we got to the sitting room, Giovanni and Rosa sat together on the sofa. He put the plasma television on with one hand and placed his arm around Rosa's shoulder.

Gianni said he had a surprise for me and went to get it. I dropped the drawing pad on the center table and was about to go to the washroom when my eyes caught the big portrait of Giovanni holding a baby, and posing with his best friend, Angelo.

"Aww, she is so cute. Was that your best friend's baby?" I asked Giovanni innocently with a smile.

He looked at the photo and gave a dismal, yes. Picking up on this I asked, "Did I say something wrong? Have you two fallen out or something?" Immediately, Giovanni let go of his wife, stood up and held my hand with reassurance.

"No you didn't say anything wrong.... and yes, that's Angelo Santiago's baby girl, Alexis. My wife took that picture of us in the hospital when she was only a day old. Do you remember, mia cara?" He asked his wife as he smiled fondly at the memory. She got up and smiled back at her husband as she cast her mind back to that moment.

"Do you remember Gianni crying because he wanted to hold the baby? He couldn't understand why we were able to carry Alexis but he was not allowed to until we promised him that when they came out of the hospital, he would get a chance to hold her; that was when he stopped crying." They both laughed then Rosa continued.

"Finally, when he held her, he fell in love with her. He was so good with her. Every day, he would insist we go over so he could hold the baby. He couldn't say her name properly so he would call her, 'Baby Ayesis.'" Giovanni and Rosa laughed again at the fond memory and so did I.

"Victoria used to say that she had found the perfect husband for Alexis and that Gianni would take very good care of her daughter. Even when they were toddlers, Gianni was so protective of her. We used to joke and say that Alexis was his first true love until he met you, of course," she said holding my hands.

Just then, Gianni came back into the room with boxes of wrapped gifts for me.

"Per te bella - for you, beautiful," he said all cheery and handed the boxes to me.

"Kind, Sir, you shouldn't have," I said theatrically taking the box from him with excitement like a child; then I paused and looked into his eyes.

"Gracie, Tesoro - thank you, darling," I kissed him and put the boxes on the side table. I excused myself as I rushed off to the washroom.

On my way back to the sitting room, I heard Rosa telling them that there was something very special about me and that she kept getting very strong feelings but she couldn't put all the pieces together.

"Then I saw this," she said picking up the painting with my mom in it.

Giovanni took it from her hand abruptly. He looked shocked as if he had seen a ghost; for a moment, he viewed the picture closely. Gianni observed his parents and realized something was not quite right.

"What is it? What's wrong, Papa?" He asked.

But his dad was still glaring at the picture and asked Rosa with his voice slightly shaking, "Did Sandra paint this?"

"Yes," she replied.

Gianni inspected the picture amazed.

"Wow! I didn't know she could paint; she is really good....wow! I wonder who the blonde lady is; she looks kind of familiar," he said taking the picture from his dad. He spotted me at the door.

"I didn't know you could paint. These are great! Who is the lady in the picture?" He walked towards me handing over the painting.

Rosa and Giovanni turned and looked at me in anticipation for an answer. I looked at them strangely then I replied casually,

"My mom."

Unaware of the impact of my answer, I went to open my presents. Giovanni and Rosa were taken aback. Gianni and I looked at them puzzled.

"Could it be? Is it even possible? I dare not think," he said holding his wife close.

"What? What isn't possible and why are you staring at me like that?" I asked feeling a bit perturbed. Giovanni edged forward and held my shoulders and asked me in all seriousness, "Now principessa – princess, please, I need you to think carefully; are you sure of what you are saying?"

"Come on, dad! If she says it's her mom, it is," Gianni said to his dad. Giovanni let go of me and looked at his wife. Gianni put his arm around me reassuringly. "Sorry, Sandra, my husband didn't mean to come on you too strong. It's just that it's important we know if what you are saying is correct; that's all," she said apologizing.

"Yes, she is my mother; she and my dad were murdered in our house in Mayfair when I was two years old," I replied.

Rosa collapsed; Gianni and his dad rushed over automatically to her aid amidst calling her name. Gianni called the maid to get some water while Giovanni was fanning her. I stood there frozen. I got so scared that I thought she was dead. I went and sat on the sofa, clutched the cushion and rocked myself back and forth.

"Not again; not again; no!" I kept murmuring.

Gianni came over to me stroking my hair seeing how distraught I was. I started to cry.

"She will be fine. Hey, don't cry. Look, she's fine. She just fainted and that happens sometimes....see, she is fine," he said.

I looked up and saw Giovanni giving her water to drink then he helped her up and the two of them came over to us. Gianni kissed my forehead lovingly. I rushed over to Rosa as I felt relieved that she was okay. I gave her a big hug and held her so tight.

"I am fine. I was just bowled over by what you said; that's all," she assured.

"Everyone I loved in the past died on me so I thought…" I couldn't finish what I was saying and started crying again.

"Oh! Darling, I am so sorry for scaring you," she said holding me tighter.

"I can't begin to imagine what you must have gone through all these years," she started to cry, too.

Concerned, Gianni stood up not quite sure what was happening as he watched the two women he loves the most crying. He looked over at his dad who was also very emotional. Giovanni walked over to me with tears of joy.

"Is that really you, Alexis? Il mio bellissimo Alexis – my beautiful little Alexis?" He asked.

"Oh! This is truly a miracle! Praise God in the highest."

He gave me a big hug while I stood there confused. I glanced at Rosa who held her hands to her mouth as she was overwhelmed with joy. I looked over at Gianni who stood there stupefied and staring at me.

"Alexis?" He called out almost in a whisper walking towards us with confusion in his eyes.

"My name is Sandra; I am not Alexis. I need to get some air," I said incredulously.

I did not want to hear any more so I left and went outside. I walked to the stables to see Sebastian. So many thoughts ran through my mind; could it be true? Are they the missing link to my family? Am I ready to know who I truly am? What if I am this Alexis; then what? Does this mean I am from a mafia family, too? Is that what killed my parents? Do I have any other living relatives? Grandma Faye always said that God works in mysterious ways but this would be incredible.

I started talking to the horse while rubbing his head. It just stared at me as if it was listening to what I was saying. I didn't realize it had gotten so late. It was dark and I got a bit scared being out there; I was getting cold, too. Then I heard someone coming into the stable.

"Alexis?" called Gianni shining the torch around.

"My name is Sandra," I said in defiance coming out of the shadow.

"Sorry, I mean Sandra; you must be cold," he said putting my jacket on me.

We headed back to the house without uttering a word. When we got in, his mom and dad were sitting down on the chair but got up as soon as we entered. Seeing how worried they were, I lowered my head.

"I am sorry for walking out like that," I said feeling bad. Rosa rushed over to me with her arms stretched wide.

"Oh! Darling, it's perfectly alright; we understand," she replied.

"It is too much for us to take in. I can't imagine how it must be for you. Come and sit down. Do you want something to eat?" I shook my head while sitting down on the sofa next to her; how could I possibly eat anything when my stomach was in knots?

"We've got some family albums for you to look at if you're up for it. I know you have a lot of questions you want to ask but we will take it as slow as you like," she said holding the album on her lap.

Gianni came and sat next to me while Giovanni sat next to Rosa. I took the album from her and just stared at it not sure whether or not to open it because I knew that once I did, there was no going back. Everyone waited in anticipation.

"You know, this album has not been opened for the past twenty years. Perhaps we are rushing her into this; maybe we should wait until tomorrow morning when everyone has had a goodnight's sleep," said Giovanni to Rosa.

"No, I won't sleep tonight if I don't do this," I said.

"I have been running away in finding out the truth all these years. I think it's time I stopped running."

With a deep breath, I opened the album. On the first page was written, "The Santiago Family Album." The middle had a heart-shaped photo of my mom, a baby, and Angelo. I looked through the photo album as Rosa and Giovanni explained each photo. I saw a picture of the two families on a holiday together. It seemed the Canuti and Santiago families were really close.

I saw a picture of my grandparents. I saw our homes in Mayfair, New York, and Italy. There was a picture of Gianni's grandpa with my grandpa. In their suit and hat, they really looked like mobs. Giovanni told me that the Santiago family was the head of the mobs until my great grandpa, Luigi, died. He handed it over to the Canuti family as he disowned his only son, Giuseppe, because he got married to Olivia, an African-American.

I thought that was really harsh but Giovanni explained that those days, it was a taboo. As such, my grandpa brought disgrace to the family name. Consequently, great grandpa, Luigi, and the family never forgave him for it. After the death of Luigi, Luciano Canuti took over as ordered by Luigi. However, as the new head of the mob, the first thing Luciano did was bring back his best friend, Giuseppe, into the business but Giuseppe's heart was not in it; not after he had experienced life outside of the gangster lifestyle. Things were not all that great for him and Olivia but they were happy and very much in love; he chose love over money and power.

Above all, he always tried to protect her from all the unpleasantness and antagonism from everyone. Luciano tried his best to protect them both. When Giuseppe and Olivia had a son called Angelo, he suggested to Luciano about going legitimate but Luciano opposed the idea. Since he did not want to lose his best friend, he said he would think about it. Little over a year after, Luciano also had a son and named him Giovanni after his dad. He loved his son so much that he could not bear the thought of any harm befalling him. He then understood why Giuseppe wanted to go legit. It was not as easy or straightforward as they hoped as they found it difficult to get out.

The Canutis and Santiagos felt that the only alternative was to send their sons, Giovanni and Angelo, to a boarding school in London to keep them out of the family business. Angelo graduated as a lawyer and Giovanni as an accountant who went on for his Masters in Public Relations. Giovanni married Rose, though he called her Rosa, at a very young age because she got pregnant at eighteen.

Giovanni's dad, Luciano, was against the marriage as Rosa was not a catholic. She was a Baptist and he felt his son was too young to get married but he went against his dad's counsel and married Rosa. Unfortunately, that put a strain on their relationship as father and son. After his graduation, Angelo met Victoria and they later got married giving birth to Alexandra.

The two families were overjoyed as everything was going well. Angelo had his law firm that was doing great. Victoria's modelling career was at its peak; and Giovanni had a PR firm; those were happy times. Then came the turf war that resulted in the shooting of Olivia who took the bullet for her husband and died instantly. The families went and avenged her death but it did not end there. In retaliation, they killed Angelo and Victoria who could not get away in time to Italy as the Canuti family did. No one knew what happened to Alexis, their daughter, as the body was never found.

Luciano and Giuseppe came to London as soon as they heard what happened. They searched everywhere but to no avail. Giuseppe locked up the house and moved back to Italy where he lived in recluse. The only person he saw was his best friend, Luciano, who flew from New York to see him from time to time.

After Gianni's dad was done explaining the history to me, it all became too real I could tell that the missing link in my life had finally come together. I wondered for a moment how Grandma Faye did not see a missing child in the news after the killing of my parents. I closed the album and brought it to my chest.

"So is my grandpa still alive?" I asked.

"Yes," replied Giovanni.

"Have I got other living relatives?" I asked.

"I think so but I can't be too sure. I know your great grandma is still alive and lives with him. After we moved to Italy, we lived a quiet life and did not come back to London until Gianni was sixteen. Then, my dad felt it was safe for us to return. When Gianni completed university, he joined the firm which grew pretty quickly and we expanded globally," he explained. "The Santiago and Canuti families together at last; we will become one after generations of friendship. I am so happy," he said with pride.

"I want to see my grandpa and great grandma. How old are they?" I asked.

"I know Giuseppe is one year older than my dad so he should be sixty-eight but your great grandma, I'm not so sure but she should be nearly ninety; her name is Maria," he replied.

"Wow!" I said, taking it all in. I felt like flying to Italy straight away.

"I know it's a lot to take in and you have a lot of questions you want to ask him. He will be so pleased to know you are alive," said Rosa.

"This is the most extraordinary thing to happen to our families and God be praised!" Exclaimed Rosa. "My heart is filled with joy......and to now have you as my own daughter is more than I could ever wish for." She moved closer, sat on the other side and held my hands. "For years, the Lord showed me a vision of my son's wife which is you. I could not really understand at the time. I even began to doubt a bit especially when it looked like you and my son would never get it together. I kept seeing the same vision and when I finally met you for the first time, I had a tremendous feeling towards you. I loved you as if I had known you all your life," she said, as she smiled lovingly. She then hugged me and Gianni together.

"Can I call him? Is it late to call?" I asked impatiently as I pulled away in a gentle manner.

Simultaneously, we all looked at the wall clock; it was 11:30 pm, and it was late.

Gianni went to the piano, and to my surprise, he started playing. We sang and danced before the Lord. I felt all the sadness and emptiness lift off me. We praised God way past midnight. It was about 2:20 am when everyone went to bed.

I woke up to find Rosa and Giovanni standing over us. I got up abruptly causing Gianni to wake up.

"I'm sorry. I know you said we are to sleep in separate rooms until we are married; we didn't mean to fall asleep, honestly," I apologized.

"Oh I know; don't mind me. I remember the last time I saw the two of you sleeping like this in Victoria's house when you were two and four years old just before… anyway, you both look as cute as you did then," she said.

I got up and greeted her good morning.

"Can I call grandpa now?" I asked excitedly.

"Yes, as soon as you have your breakfast and shower because you did not eat dinner last night," she said.

I jumped out of the sofa quickly to go and shower. After Gianni and I had breakfast, we joined his mom and dad who were waiting in the study to make the call. I was so excited and nervous. Giovanni said he needed to call his dad first in New York so his dad would call my grandpa. Otherwise, he would not take our call if we called him directly.

We gathered at the desk as Giovanni dialed the number to his dad on the silver and black videophone. He picked up and on the screen was a dashing older version of Giovanni but a lot more tanned. He was dressed in charcoal pinstripe Giorgio Armani suit with a Louis Vuitton classic dark blue silk tie. He looked so young that he could pass as an older brother to Giovanni. He answered the phone and pleased to hear from his son and even more pleased to see his grandson.

"Hello son! To what do I owe this unexpected surprise not that I'm complaining as I very rarely get calls from you."

"Papa, as far as I am concerned, that is now water under the bridge; a family is the most important thing in this life and nothing else matters," he said wanting to get to the point of his call.

His dad, astounded by what his son had said, immediately asked if all was well. After reassuring him that everything was fine, he asked his dad to sit down that he had news that would leave him dumbfounded. He brought me to the screen and asked Luciano if he knew who I was.

"Of course I do; that's Sandra, my grandson's beautiful fiancée," he replied.

"I saw her in New York when he proposed to her though she did not see me as he had not yet told her who I was. Hello Sandra, I must say I am very pleased to see you. Where is my grandson? Come closer to the screen. I am very pleased that everything has worked out for you."

I waved at him smiling then Gianni moved closer and put his arms around my waist.

"Grandpa, you have no idea," said Gianni.

"Ciao papà come stai – hello, papa, how are you?" Rosa greeted him joyfully.

"Mia bella figlia, come si osserva raggiante - my beautiful daughter, you look radiant!" He said smiling at her. He had grown to love and accept Rosa as his daughter over the years especially after giving him a grandson.

"Grazie, papa," she replied.

"Papa, a miracle has happened and I cannot wait any longer. I must tell you and mamma now!" Giovanni said impatiently like a child.

"Ciò che è mio figlio? - What is it, my son?" He asked wondering what was so pressing.

"We have found Alexis or shall I say, she found us, or rather, God brought her back to the family and much more," he exclaimed.

"Is she okay?" He asked. "Have you invited her to the house? What if she doesn't like us? Where has she been all these years? I must see her with my own eyes."

Everyone was just smiling as he asked all the questions.

"Papa, papa; you are looking at her right now," Giovanni said ecstatically putting me right in front of the screen.

"Hello," I said shyly.

"Sandra? Alexis? Alexandra Olivia Santiago? This cannot be.... can it? Is that really you?" he asked amazed.

"It is, Papa; it really is her. Praise be to God. After all these years, who would have thought she could become the wife of my son? It is beyond my wildest dreams," said Rosa. "Oh! I wish I was there with you; this is the happiest day of my life. I must call my friend," he said all excited. "I know he will not believe it until he sees her with his own eyes." He paused for a moment and with authority, commanded still with excitement, "Prepare to fly out to Italy. I will call my pilot to get the jet ready. I will meet you at the family home then we all go to the Santiago mansion. I will bring my dad; he did not think he would live to see her again. This is truly a miracle! I can't wait to see you in person, Alexandra. I must go. I have to tell your mother," he said to his son, Giovanni, with tears in his eyes.

"Okay, ciao papa. We will see you tomorrow morning. We should arrive before midday tomorrow," said Giovanni. We said goodbye and the call ended.

"Tomorrow morning? Do we have to wait that long before we go and see my grandpa? Can't we go now? I can't wait that long," I whined like a child.

He looked at Rosa and Gianni who were nodding in agreement.

"Oh! Alright, principessa – princess. We will take the private jet. We will get there in a couple of hours. I will call my dad and let him know the change of plans," he replied.

I leaped forward throwing my arms around him and thanked him.

"Oh my goodness! What shall I wear?" I asked myself rushing off with Gianni hand in hand to my room.

I could hear his mom and dad laughing behind us. But that was sorted by the presents Gianni bought for me the previous day.

"I knew you have not had time to shop for a gown and the ball is next week. It's probably the last thing on your mind but I don't want you to worry about the office; everything is running smoothly," he said.

"So that's where you and your dad went yesterday amongst buying my things for the ball? Has Annabel told Gina that she would be travelling to our Shanghai office next week Thursday?" I asked.

"No, not yet," he replied.

"Good, because I want to do that myself. I want to see her face when I tell her. That would teach her not to mess with me and my man," I said smiling deviously.

"Remind me never to mess with you," he said wrestling me to the bed playfully and tickling me.

We both rolled around the bed laughing then he paused and gazed into my eyes tenderly; then he started kissing me. I felt his hard-on so I rolled him off.

"Come on, Mr. Horny! You better go and take a cold shower," I said.

He ran his fingers through his hair quickly and rubbed his face roughly.

"We are going to have this wedding as soon as possible because I don't think I can wait this long; this is torture," he replied.

He got up reluctantly pouting like a child. He looked so cute. I could not help but kiss him lovingly on his pouting lips then sent him off to go get ready.

Chapter Four

The Santiagos

"Wow!" I exclaimed as I stood at the door of the plane. I had flown first class before but this was out of the world. I stood at the aisle with my mouth wide opened as I looked at the extravagance on display in the private jet. While his parents spoke to the pilot, Gianni gave me a tour of the plane. There was an in-plane wireless LAN and remote controlled DVD, TV, and MP3, along with bar service, Jacuzzi including bedrooms, bathrooms with full shower, conference rooms, and full-on entertainment system.

Once the plane took off, the flight attendants served a lovely gourmet lunch. Not long after, the pilot announced our arrival in Italy. As we got off the plane, I could see the beautiful blue sea and a huge mansion afar — the view was breathtakingly beautiful.

In a very short while, I would meet my grandpa and great grandma. I was so nervous as it all felt like a dream. As if reading my mind, Gianni pinched me.

"Ouch!" I cried out. He smiled taking my hand as we walked down together towards the waiting black limo. There were two other cars behind with some bodyguards also waiting; I felt like royalty. Giovanni would point and tell me stories about the land as we drove to the house. The mansion appeared humongous as we got closer. Rosa rubbed my hand, smiled and told me to relax. I smiled back still nervous. The limo stopped and the driver opened our door. As we stepped out, there were some people waiting for us. Gianni put his arms around my waist as we moved towards them. They all greeted us but not one spoke English; only Italian. As I was looking around, my eyes caught a white-haired man looking out through the window from upstairs. I guessed that must be my grandpa. I squeezed Gianni's hand to get his attention. I rolled my eyes up towards the direction of my grandpa and he followed my gaze then he nodded acknowledging him as the one. We went inside. The ceiling alone was beautifully painted with angels. Everything looked grand and glittery. I held on to Gianni's hand tightly. We sat down as some of the people that came to meet us went up the glass lift.

"He's just gone to inform Uncle Giuseppe," Giovanni turned to me and said.

It seemed like forever before he finally came down. He approached us with caution; his eyes were transfixed on me as I was the first to see him come in. Giovanni noticed me staring and followed my gaze. He stood up unreservedly to address him.

"Uncle Giuseppe!" He said, giving him a hug as did Rosa.

Gianni and I stood up and observed as we held on to each other. Gianni didn't really know him that well though he had heard a lot about him and seen him a few times. He kept staring at me then tears began to form in his eyes. Somehow, that stirred an overwhelming emotion within me as I stared back at his kind eyes. He looked so much older than Luciano even though he was only one year older. I guess that's what grief does to a person. Even though he looked old and almost frail-looking, it was evident his good looks cheated age. He walked towards me and stopped in front of me. I stood there unsure of what to do.

"Olivia, my beautiful Olivia," he said as he hugged me sobbing.

I could no longer hold my emotions; I began to sob. An old woman came in with another woman about Giovanni's age. Grandpa took me by the hand to them, "Guardate quello che Dio ha fatto la nostra Olivia è tornata a noi - look what God has done; our Olivia has come back to us," he said.

Great grandma gave me a hug and spoke Italian as did the woman with her whom I found out was my auntie. A big banquet was held in my honor. A lot of people were introduced to me as the family but it was too much for me to take in. Everybody spoke Italian and all I could do was smile. Grandpa held my hand proudly with his head high and shoulders back. It was as if the frail old man I saw moments earlier had disappeared. He looked strong and powerful with such joy and peace in his countenance. He showed me my room on the first floor which used to be my mom and dad's. It was a huge master bedroom suite. On the dressing table was a picture of my mom and dad on their wedding day; they looked so beautiful and happy. Next to it was another picture of the three of us when I was a baby. Just then, Gianni came through the door and spoke to grandpa in Italian. After a while, grandpa left.

"I leave you to change and come down. You'll find some of your mother's clothes. Wear them if you like," he said.

When he closed the door on his way out, I flopped on the bed letting out a big sigh.

"I know it's a lot to take in; you're doing great," said Gianni as he came and sat next to me taking my hand.

"Two days ago I had no family but now I have them coming out of my ears. Not that I'm complaining; I am very happy but it is a lot to take in as you said," I groaned slightly feeling a bit tired.

I laid back on the bed with my eyes closed. Gianni laid next to me. I opened them again and we were facing each other.

"I am sorry for ignoring you all day," I said.

"Don't be; this is your night. I totally understand," he replied.

"I have watched you all night; people coming over to you with great joy welcoming you back to the family; I still can't believe you are my little Alexis," Gianni said continuing with a long speech, "So many thoughts have been going through my mind. I can't believe how we ended up together even though there were so many obstacles over the years that always pulled us closer together making us stronger. I didn't think it was possible to love you more but the love in my heart for you is all-pervading. I now understand why even before we formally met, I was madly in love with you. I bought every magazine whose cover you were on; I mean you were my pin-up girl.

I couldn't believe my luck when I saw you in the nightclub for the first time but I was too awestruck to say anything. You were there with Anthony, of course; within me, I was burning with jealousy and I could not understand why. From that moment on, I tried to arrange to be wherever you were. My dad told me it was not healthy to feel that way and that I should get over my obsession and get myself a real girlfriend. He said I was turning out to be a stalker. I realized my dad was right so I started going out with Gina. But as hard as I tried, I could not get you out of my head. Gina thought I was with her for three years because I loved her but she was just a distraction. Perhaps, she picked up on that because she became very clingy and pushy but I put up with it for a while until I read the newspaper about the break-up with you and Steve. That was when I broke it off with her.

I tried in different ways to keep you in my life. L'Oréal was one of our biggest clients; I asked them if they could make you the face of L'Oréal. That way, I could see you always on TV and in the magazines." I opened my eyes in shock that he was the one responsible for getting me the L'Oreal job. At the time, I remember thinking about how my agent managed to get me such a big contract. He continued, "I got to know your agent too so I made sure you got as much modelling jobs as you wanted. I was very sad when you left L'Oréal and stopped modelling but I finally got my chance when I arranged for you to model at the ball the night we met. I was so nervous though I had rehearsed that moment so many times over the years. I wanted it to be perfect and it was. You were everything I had dreamed of and more," he stroked my face tenderly.

"The first time we made love was magical. It felt as if we had known each other all our lives. From that moment, I knew I could not live without you. I could not explain it but there was such a powerful connection between us; now, I know why." His face changed to a sad expression looking up at the ceiling. "The shock you gave me that first morning you turned up for work as Gina introduced you as the new temp...I could not believe it." He turned to face me again with a happier expression. "We have come a long way since then and nothing will come between us again; no more secrets," he said, looking into my eyes.

I was totally speechless. I stood up backing him as I walked over to the handcrafted lead glass French door that opened to the master bedroom and a spectacular master bathroom featuring the finest granite and marble; Swarovski crystal pulls and knobs, European fixtures, Jacuzzi and bidet. I tried to admire the beauty of the place so I didn't have to process all that he had just revealed. He came and turned me around to face him.

"I know my behavior at that time was obsessive and frightening but I promise you I'm not that kind of person. To be quite honest with you, I was frightened too but I could not bring myself to stop. It was like I was driven by a force beyond my control but it all makes sense now. I just feel so relieved because I did not know who that person was," he said.

"I am telling you all this because I want you to know all of me:

the good and the bad. I broke my virginity when…"

"Eh! Let's not go there," I said stopping him from going any further.

I walked back and sat on the dressing table. I looked at myself in the mirror regretting the promiscuous life I had led and all the drunken binges I had before and after university. It probably would have been worse if I didn't have Anthony at the time. I sighed and said, "If you know so much about me, then you must also know I am no shrinking violet when it comes to men." I stood up and walked towards the window. He came behind me and put his hands around my waist and kissed my neck.

"I don't care if you have had a thousand men. If you ask me, the more the experience, the better; you are so great in bed," he said nuzzling my neck.

I turned to face him hitting him in the arm playfully, "Come on; be serious," I said.

"I am being serious; you are great in bed and an incredible kisser. Why do you think I can't keep my hands off you?" He replied.

"Aaahh, so that is why you are with me, huh?" I asked teasing him.

"Amongst other things," he replied pulling me closer to him.

Just as I thought he was about to kiss me, he got all serious and said, "ti amo, Alexandra."

I looked at him thinking I would feel weird with him calling me that but somehow it felt right — everything felt just right. After I got ready, we went to his suite which was next to mine where he changed clothes. We both went back downstairs where everyone was rejoicing and celebrating. Giovanni and Rosa were on the dance floor. My grandpa was dancing with great grandma. Gianni and I went and got a glass of champagne and watched everyone as they made merry. Grandpa saw me and Gianni and came over. He took my hand asking me to join him; we danced as more people joined us on the dance floor, with everyone smiling at us and waving. We sat down in the corner after and just chatted about what I thought of the family. People would come over speaking Italian as we were there. Some of the younger ones tried speaking English for my benefit. I didn't realize how late it was until Luciano and his wife, Carmella, arrived with his dad. Upon seeing them, grandpa stood up with his arms opened to embrace them. I stood up and Carmella embraced me with a kiss on both cheeks. The party went on until the early hours of the morning. I finally went to bed exhausted about 4 am.

By the time I woke up, got ready and went downstairs, it was nearly 2 pm. Grandpa and Gianni were sitting down outside on the veranda. It was such a lovely sunny day; the maid took me where they were sitting. As I approached, they both stood up like the gentlemen they were. Gianni pulled out my chair for me to sit down. After we ate, grandpa gave Gianni and me a tour of the whole estate including the huge vineyard and olive grove. Back in the house, I noticed he had a lot of paintings.

Like me, he loved painting and was an art collector, too.

"But I enjoyed the beauty as a part of my lifestyle," he would say.

He explained that sometimes, he bought the paintings to fill the void he felt in his life; after the death of his wife, son and daughter-in-law and the mysterious disappearance of his granddaughter whom everyone believed was also dead. Grandma Olivia used to paint so the paintings, he was convinced, brought him closer to her. When he realized I could paint, he couldn't hide his delight. He took us to his private study where he stayed most of the time to escape from everyone and everything. The study was like a big library filled with art collections. There was a big portrait of grandpa with grandma on their wedding day. They looked so happy and next to it was another with my dad, Angelo; and then a big one of all of us. My mom and dad were sitting down with me, two years then, on daddy's lap, then grandma and grandpa stood behind us; and on top was written, The Santiago Family. I stared at that picture for a long time.

I felt a great deal of sadness and let out a deep sigh; Gianni put his arms around me. I lowered my head and wished that my parents were still alive. Grandpa came to me, took my hands and said, "Il mio bambino - my child, do not be sad for God has comforted us by your return; we all believed you were dead, too....but the Lord, out of His infinite mercy, spared your life and miraculously brought you back to us." I looked up at him and tried to smile as I hid the pain I felt in my heart. He continued, "I know you miss them but we are all here for you now; hmm, mia bella figlia - my beautiful daughter, we are here for you."

He hugged me as my eyes were filled with tears. We walked back to his grand exquisite traditional-styled office furniture and sat down on the luxurious office chairs next to his desk. He sat on his desk where I asked him to tell me more about my parents. He took out a small key from his desk, drew and unlocked the bottom drawer and brought out a brown envelope and a photo album. He carefully opened the brown envelope as Gianni and I watched.

He handed over a gold locket with the inscription, Santiago Family. I opened it and it was a picture of my parents on their wedding day and the one opposite was a picture of me with a big smile. He said it was a gift for my mom from my dad when she gave birth to me. He handed me my birth certificate. Upon looking, I realized my real birthday was March 28. He then brought out the family album with pictures of my dad's childhood, grandma and her siblings, my cousins and nephews.

According to his narration, when my dad graduated, he started a law firm called Santiago Law Firm which was now a world-class international law firm; the same law firm Mandy worked for; I couldn't believe it — this is truly a small world. And after his death, grandma's younger brother was put in charge. Grandpa put in place people who ran the family businesses and his friend, Luciano, kept him updated about things that he needed to know.

There was a black and white picture of great grandma, Maria, with great grandpa, Luigi, when they were younger; maybe in their 30s.

The more grandpa told me about our family history, the more I felt like a Santiago. I sat back on the chair thinking how wonderful it was to finally be home at last with my own blood family who loved me so much. There was such a sense of relief, not only did I have my family who loved me, I had the Canuti family, too. The joy was so overwhelming that I could not hide it even if I tried. I did not even know when I started laughing.

"And what could be funny?" Grandpa asked bringing me to consciousness.

I explained to him that I was just happy to have such a wonderful family and I was even more blessed to be getting married in a wonderful and close family. I held Gianni's hand and smiled. He smiled back and expressed how honored he was to have such great in-laws who were already a family to us. A call came through and we left to meet Gianni's grandpa and his wife, Carmella, in the living room. Their faces lit up as we entered; after a while sitting and watching television together, we were famished. So at the invitation to come over for dinner, we ran as fast as a deer in search of water in the desert.

We both looked at each other and giggled childishly while the others looked on and laughed.

The layout was a classic wooden Italian dining set. Once we were all seated and the drinks were served, Luciano picked up the champagne glass, held it up and said, "A Dio onnipotente ea voi preziosi Alexandra - To God Almighty and to you precious Alexandra." After toasting, we drank the champagne.

"Aaahh, the best champagne in the world," said Luciano jestingly.

"After Santiago champagne, of course," said Grandpa Giuseppe joining in the fun.

"Of course," laughed Luciano.

"The two of you will never change," said Carmella playfully.

The two friends laughed toasting to each other. Gianni and I looked at each other, smiling and enjoying the whole scene. The meal was delicious. When the meal was over, we went for a stroll in the night-lit garden pond. We walked and talked for about thirty minutes then went back to the house. Luciano, grandpa, and Carmella were practically exhausted. We left them in the living room and decided to go for a swim in the pool. Gianni's grandparents had gone back home when we went back inside. Grandpa was waiting for us. He told us we would spend the next day at the Canuti estate.

In the morning after breakfast, I got ready and we left after lunchtime. Gianni came to my room to tell me to take a few more clothes as I would spend a couple of days there before coming back. As I packed, I noticed he was rather excited. He simply couldn't wait to show me his house and I was not disappointed when he did. It was a mega-mansion that sat on acres of land with aristocratic beauty and an incomparable quality.

Rosa and Giovanni were with the oldies in the screening room; they left a message for us to meet them there after we had eaten. When we got there, they were watching family films; we watched the films until about 1:30 am before we went to bed. I saw a picture of my dad from when granny Olivia was pregnant; also when he and Giovanni graduated and got married.

Seeing photos was one thing but watching everything on the screen was phenomenal. I kept saying to myself, "I am Alexis Santiago." The films also showed me how deep and close the friendship between the Santiago and Canuti was and how extraordinary it was that we were to be united as one family in marriage. Before we headed off to bed, we agreed on how and when to announce my return to the family to the media. Luciano and grandad decided we should keep it within the family until they both went back to New York to test the waters. They were both fearful of what might happen especially grandpa. Though they felt it was safe, they wanted to be 100 percent sure.

Rosa and I went horse riding in the morning. We went to the gym for a light workout then shower; I felt relaxed but very hungry. My late breakfast was served outside in the glistening pool and patio with an outstanding view. Rosa joined me for breakfast. We discussed the wedding and when and where we would get wedded. Gianni joined us but he asked to leave soon after as he was visiting Giovanni at the office so I requested to go with him.

Gianni decided to take me out to a late lunch so we left his dad in the office and went out. After our meal, he took me around to show me the town — we had such a great time. By the time we got home, it was late but grandpa Giuseppe and Luciano were at the bar so we joined them. He expressed that he had almost forgotten what it felt like to live. My resurfacing did give grandpa every reason to live. Old age and loneliness were no longer his weakness.

"I feel like a young man," he said holding his fist up playfully jabbing Gianni's tummy like a boxer. Gianni pulled back playfully as if in pain.

"Easy, Tyson; you might do him some real damage," said Luciano and we burst out laughing.

Gianni went to the bar and fixed us some drinks. We sat up and joked and laughed until very late. It was really nice spending time with grandpa and Gianni's grandpa; they were quite fun. Grandpa was so much happier and a lot more jovial which was great to see. I was quite tired so after my drink, I kissed them goodnight and went to bed.

I woke up late in the morning which meant that horse-riding with Rosa was off the cards. I had a light workout in the gym instead then went for a swim. After all that, I had some food then took the elevator back to my room. I had a bit of time to myself as it had been a go, go, and go for a long time. I just sat down on the sofa and put my feet up and turned on the television. I got my mobile phone and checked it; I had so many missed calls and text messages from Mandy and one from Anthony and Tracey. I also got a message from Mrs. Abbott: she wanted to know how I got on and if Gianni and I had sorted out our differences. I called Annabel to make sure she sent Mrs. Abbott her flight tickets for her birthday and to fill me in on what had been going on since I left the office. I called Mandy next. She just kept screaming in my ear on how many times she had tried calling me and how unfair it was for me to take off like that without letting her know where I was.

I apologized to her and told her that I was fine and everything was fine.

"I called Anthony and he said you had to get away for a few days to clear your head about things but this is more than a few days, Sandra," she said with an angry tone, "I mean the ball is in a few days and we have not even gone shopping like we normally would do to get our outfits; oh! By the way, I am now out of the hospital and I am totally fine."

Mandy kept on blabbing, "Anyway, when are you coming back? You are still going to the ball, aren't you? Please say you are because I have really been looking forward to this and with makeup, you can't even see my bruises; how great is that?" Before I could answer, she continued: "Have you sorted things out with your mafia boyfriend? Ha! I still can't believe Gianni is from one of the richest families in the world. Wow! Sandra, you really hit the jackpot there....minus the mafia and he would totally be a perfect boyfriend. So when are you coming back?" Again I tried to answer but she continued: "Oh, by the way, Joanna has been trying to buy her way back into our good books and she has been begging us to talk to you. Sandra? Are you still there? Sandra!" She yelled.

It was good to hear her sounding like her old self again but I wondered whether she and Aden were still together after what he did to her.

"Yes," I answered, missing her banter and happy that she was out of the hospital and feeling much better.

"What was the last thing I said?" She asked disbelieving that I was listening.

"You said that Joanne was trying to worm her way back with expensive gifts," I replied.

"Oh! Alright then, when are you coming back? I miss you already. We have a lot to catch up on," she whined.

"You have no idea!" I exclaimed.

"What? Has something happened?" She asked concerned.

"Don't worry. I will fill you in when I come back at some point tomorrow or the day after. Are you back at work now?" I asked wondering how she would take it finding out she works for me.

"No, I'll go back on Monday," she replied.

I asked her if she had heard from Aden. She said she didn't want to talk about it on phone and that she would tell me when I come back to London. After speaking with Mandy, I called and left a message for Mrs. Abbott wishing her happy birthday and telling her that all was more than fine with me. Lastly, I called Annabel and told her I would be in the office on Thursday as the ball was on Saturday to make sure everything was in order. When I finished making all my calls, I went up to check if Rosa was in her room; she was not so I decided to go for a walk in the beautiful garden.

After my walk, I saw grandpa coming back with Luciano in a car; I ran to him and gave them a cuddle; they were so happy to see me. We went back inside together. Luciano told me that his son and grandson went to the office and he and my grandad were just coming back from one of the branches of Santiago Law Firm and some of our other businesses. Grandpa informed me that they needed to make some changes. When I asked if I could go to the see my dad's law firm, they said it would have to be another day as we were all going out later on the Santiago yacht for dinner which was a formal event.

I told grandpa that I had nothing formal to wear but he said I was not to worry. He went behind the grand piano and took out a big white long box prettily wrapped in a big red bow and handed it over to me.

"This was your grandmother's. I gave it to her on our last wedding anniversary, the night I surprised her with her yacht Olivia. I would be very honored if you would wear it tonight if it's not weird for you. I would understand if it is," he said.

I took the box and kissed him on the cheek thanking him. I walked over to the chair and put the box on the table and opened it. In it was a beautiful red gown. I lifted it up and put it against my body as I admired the beauty of the handmade button for the see-through back, French lace with a sequence elegant train. The style was almost Chinese with silk inside and the lace outside the dress was absolutely stunning. I could imagine grandma in that dress. I hugged grandpa.

"I would be honored to wear it," I told him.

He gave me the shoe and handbag to match. I was so happy; my first gift from a member of my family. I felt a bit emotional about it for some reason. I took my gifts upstairs to my room and went to the spa. I wanted to look stunning to outdo the gracefulness of the dress.

Chapter Five

There's a God

"Mamma mia!" Exclaimed Luciano.

"You can say that again," said Carmella with a beaming smile.

"Mamma mia," echoed Giovanni.

"You look like Auntie Olivia," he said.

"You look amazing," said Rosa.

"Guardate mio figlio, lei sembra proprio come il vostro Olivia - Look, my son, she looks just like your Olivia," said great-grandmother, Maria, elbowing grandpa.

"Sì mama, sì- Yes, mum; yes," he said filled with emotions.

"Beh andare in figlio Non state lì a sbavare, aiutare la bella signora le scale – Well, go on, son, don't stand there drooling; help the beautiful lady down the stairs," laughed his great grandad, Giovanni, pushing Gianni forward.

I stood at the top of the stairs momentarily watching my new family; they all looked great. I was so filled with joy and was thankful to God in my heart for his blessings. I made my way gracefully down the stairs with care feeling like a princess as all eyes were on me. I looked at each and every one of their faces and all had the expression of adoration. Gianni ran midway to escort me down the stairs like the perfect prince he was; my Prince Charming. Then he whispered close to my ear, "You look hot."

"You look hot, too," I replied softly.

Carmella commented on how much I looked like Olivia, my grandmother.

"You can say that again. For a moment, I thought I was seeing a ghost," said Luciano.

Grandpa stretched out his hands towards me and held my hands almost in tears, "You have made an old man very happy. Thank you, Cara," said grandpa.

"Hey, you are still a young man, nonno - Grandpa," I said smiling.

When I finally got down, I kissed him and everyone else on the cheek. After all the exchange of pleasantries, we made our way to the stretched black limos parked outside which took us out to the yacht. The yacht was really big. We had the crew waiting for us as we arrived. The yacht must have been about seventy meters long. I could see on the side written in gold on the white vessel, Olivia, with the Santiago logo by the side. I was already impressed by the beauty of the yacht until we went inside; it was like a floating palace. Gold, marble and other expensive materials along with mahogany furniture were used in the decoration of the luxurious yacht. It was simply exquisite.

The musicians were playing a sweet classical piece by Wolfgang Amadeus Mozart. The nine of us sat down around the beautiful well-decorated dining table and the crew began to serve drinks. The champagne that was served was, of course, Canuti champagne and as always, the two best friends, grandpa and Luciano, made their usual joke of whom made the best wine. We toasted to the upcoming wedding and the family. The two families chatted excitedly and Gianni and I kept looking at each other grinning happily.

All of a sudden, great grandmother Maria started laughing out loud. We turned to her wondering what was so funny.

"Vi sbagliate le mie gambe per il mio bisnonno-figlia giovane, io sono lusingato - you mistaken my legs for my great grand-daughter, young man; I am flattered," she said to Gianni.

Gianni blushed and everyone started laughing. I looked at grandpa for translation which he did; then I started laughing too. Gianni also saw the funny side of it and started to laugh.

Wedding plans followed right after dinner. We agreed to have the wedding in Italy and fly the guests from abroad. Rosa and great grandmother, Maria, insisted we have the ceremony in church though grandpa wanted it in our estate. We resolved to have the ceremony in the church and the reception at our estate. Now, all what remained was to pick a date. This took a while as we could not agree; some wanted it after the harvest, while others wanted it in the spring to give us more time to prepare. I did not want a winter wedding and Gianni did not want to wait a moment longer. We finally reached a suitable date which was four weeks ahead; just a month before harvest when the weather would still be warm.

The music started to play again and Gianni took my hand to dance. We waltzed for what seemed like hours — it was so romantic.

"I cannot wait for you to finally be Mrs. Alexandra Canuti," he said. I couldn't believe either that I was getting married in four weeks. I couldn't wait to tell Mandy.

We did not stay too late because we were flying back to London in the early hours of the morning and I would go back to the office. The driver dropped us at ours while the other limo took Luciano's dad back to the Canuti estate. Luciano and Carmella with grandad were coming to London with us then after the ball on Saturday, they would head back to New York.

The jet landed at the Canuti estate in Surrey, by 7 am. We had breakfast on the plane so I put on some of the new office clothes I bought in Italy and was ready for the office. The car picked us up and drove us to the house but Gianni and I left for the office while the rest stayed behind. They were going to meet us later in the evening in London or perhaps drop by at the office, if possible. Before nine o'clock, we were at the office. Some people were already there. I went to my office and saw everything was in tip top shape as if I had never been away. I was a bit disappointed but at the same time happy to know the business ran smoothly with or without me there. Gianni went to his office and not long after that, Annabel came in. The place started to fill up. The usual hustle and bustle of the office began.

Many were surprised to see me back as they were not sure when I was due back; I even heard a rumor that I had left the company. Gina was not at all pleased to see me though she tried to mask it unsuccessfully. She didn't waste any time at all; I saw her heading towards Gianni's office. I went to be at the door to listen in for a while. I heard her making her usual threats to Gianni; how she would reveal his identity to me. Gianni just looked at her in a nonchalant manner, ignored her and went back to work. That infuriated her.

"Did you hear what I just said?" she demanded, "I am not joking. I am going to march right over to her office now and tell her everything and that would be the end of the two of you."

"You know, Gina, I think your time in this office is up. You forget that I am your boss and not the other way round," Gianni got up to say.

"Oh! Don't bother with the threats. You can't get rid of me that easily. If you could, you would have done it by now," she said smugly.

"You forget who you are talking to," he said coldly leaning forward with his hands on his desk. Just then I barged in.

"Don't you knock? Can't you see we are having a private meeting?" she turned around and snapped.

"First of all, Gina, I don't appreciate the manner you have just used on me and secondly, I can walk into this office anytime I want without knocking as Gianni is my fiancé. His office is my office; get used to it," I said walking over to Gianni.

"Not if I have anything to do with it," she murmured.

"What was that?" I asked.

"I said I understand," she said reluctantly. Ss she was about to go, I called her back. She turned and looked at me waiting to hear what I had to say.

"Something has come up at our Shanghai office and we need one of our most experienced staff to fly out there immediately," I said.

Her face lit up a bit because I know she always wanted to go to our international offices but she never got the chance. "When do I leave, Monday?" she asked smiling.

I could barely contain myself. I looked at Gianni who kept a straight face and didn't want to look at me because he would burst out laughing. I regarded her for a moment, "You leave this evening," I said.

She was completely flummoxed by what I said.

"This evening?" she asked with an outburst.

"Yes," I replied with a stern expression and loving every minute of it because I knew what was going through her mind that moment. She began to give me reasons to why she could not leave the night.

"You can do half day; that will give you enough time to pack a small bag. You are not staying long since you should be back by Tuesday," I said helping her out.

"Tuesday?" she asked surprised she was coming back so soon.

"Oh I get it. You just want to get me out of the way so I will miss the ball but your little game is not going to work. Tell her, Gianni," she said looking at him for support but he clearly stated to her that

I was the manager and whatever decision I made was final. She was peeved.

"Are you saying you don't want to work for the company anymore? Because your refusal to go to Shanghai clearly means you no longer wish to work for us. You might as well go and clear your desk out now," I said rubbing it in.

"You would just love that, wouldn't you? But I will not give you the satisfaction. Okay, I will play your game, little girl; but know this, you will live to regret it," she said precariously.

"Your days are numbered here, Gina. Mark my words. Now run along and get your flight itinerary from Annabel. She will arrange for a driver to pick you to your house to pack a few things and then take you to the airport to ensure you get on the plane safely. We wouldn't want anything happening to you hence preventing you from traveling this evening; do we, dearie?" I said mordantly giving her a sardonic grin. As she turned to go tightening her jaws, I called her back.

"Oh Gina, one more thing," she turned grudgingly facing me, "I hope you didn't go through too much trouble buying an outfit for the ball on Saturday; it can be quite a costly affair."

She took a deep breath and asked me if there was anything else. When I said no, she left the office seething. I turned to Gianni who could not keep a straight face any longer.

"You are scary," he said holding my waist and turning me around to face him.

"Yeah, and don't you forget it," I said poking his nose with my index finger gently. He purred like a tiger.

"Have I told you how hot you look?" He said pulling me closer to him seductively.

"Mm…down boy, we have a lot of work to catch up on especially me. I need to round up in case I will not be working here much longer," I said pulling away.

Before I closed the door behind me, I looked at him standing with a big grin. I shook my head smiling then closed the door. I went back to my office and called Annabel. We went through everything including the preparation for the ball on Saturday. I asked her if she was bringing her boyfriend. She told me they broke up and that she was bringing her mom instead.

Grandpa rang me to say that he was unable to make it to the office during the day so we arranged that he would come to my flat instead. After work, I did some grocery shopping because I wanted to cook something nice for grandpa. While I was in the supermarket, Mandy rang and I told her I would definitely drop by her house later on in the night or some point tomorrow to give her the present I bought for her from Italy. I called Anthony to let him know I was back and that we had a lot to catch up on but we had to do it face to face. I asked him if he was still coming to the ball. He was not too keen, however, I persuaded him to. I requested of him to bring his mom and dad that their names were on the guest list. He enquired if I had worked things out with Gianni. I told him that everything was fine. When I questioned if he had seen Joanne, he replied he had not, since that day. I assured him that what happened between him and Joanne was water under the bridge and that we should all move on.

I called Tracy after to make sure she and her husband were still coming on Saturday. She said they were and she was happy to know that everything was fine between Gianni and me. She was also happy to know that Anthony and I were still friends. I wanted to find out whether she had spoken to Joanne, but she informed me that she had been busy but saw few missed calls from her. I encouraged her to forgive Joanne as she was just being who she is. Hopefully, that experience taught her a lesson.

I called Joanne, the phone did not ring long before she answered it as she was surprised but pleased that I called. Immediately, she began to apologize again asking for my forgiveness. I informed her that I had forgiven her and as far as I was concerned, it was all in the past. I instructed her that I was expecting her at the Canuti ball on Saturday which really made her day. After speaking with all my friends, I felt so much better. Everything in my life for once was uncomplicated.

It was good to be back in my flat again. It felt as if I had been away for months. I put the food on the fire and went to have a quick shower. After that, I called grandpa to know where he was and what time he was coming. He was five minutes away. I laid the food on the table and a little excited he was coming to see my flat. Not long after, my doorbell rang. Once he was inside, he had a good look around the flat. He was impressed with it which made me happy. We sat and ate our dinner; after which we sat on the sofa and talked about our day and how it went.

I asked him how he felt about coming back to London after all those years. He expressed how strange it was at first coming back without his son and daughter-in-law but he had me so it was not all that bad. He told me he went to the city to visit our law firm, met the workers and the person in charge of the London branch.

"I told Alan Graham, the branch manager, that there were going to be some changes and I would call for a meeting sometime next week so that I could introduce you to them once we go public about your real identity but that would be when I come back from New York."

"Whatever you feel is best, Nonno – Grandpa; but I don't know anything about being a lawyer," I said with angst-ridden expression.

"No. You don't have to be a lawyer mia figlia - my daughter, you are the boss and that is that," he said loving every minute of me being his grand-daughter. Frankly, I was loving having him as my granddad.

"Wow!" I said sitting back.

"There is more I want to introduce you to; Maxwell Fairfax is our property developer here in London. He is in charge of our property firm; the bank of Santiago is our bank, vineyard and olive grove, the art collections plus all the investments including bonds, stocks, and shares. I think that pretty much covers the family business." He held my hand and patted it in a gentle manner. "Everything is now yours; you do with it what you will; you are the heiress to the Santiago fortune and I am pleased to know that no one would try to seduce you into marriage to get their hands on the fortune. Our God is merciful!" he said smiling joyfully.

"Nonno, do you know that Maxwell Fairfax is the dad of one of my friends? And my best friend, Mandy, works for our law firm in the city? Mamma mia, this is really a small world," I said amazed. Grandpa and I spoke for a little while longer. I showed him the spare room for him to sleep. I texted Mandy to see her tomorrow, then went to bed.

Friday was a very busy day in the office. We closed early because of the ball the day ahead. I barely saw Gianni all day and the office was a lot friendlier without Gina. I went to Mandy's in the afternoon straight from work. She was so happy to see me as was her parents. I was surprised to see her older sister there. She ran off when she was 15 years old with her much older boyfriend and broke her parents' heart. Mandy did not talk about her so I'd always presumed Mandy was an only child. It wasn't too long ago that Mandy mentioned her briefly in our conversation when she was hospitalized. Her sister was quiet throughout, almost unfriendly to me even though we just met. The house was not as lively as it used to be. Looking at Mandy, I could see she was not too pleased having to move back home again. I wondered if that meant Aden and her were over for good. I was quite relieved when Mandy and I went to her room; she closed the door behind her.

"Peace at last!" she sighed walking over to me and slumped on the bed. I put my bag on her dressing table and sat on the chair next to her bed. Turning to me, she said, "Don't get me wrong; I love my family but it's hard to have your own privacy at times. I really would love to get my own place but to get a nice decent flat is very expensive; I would need a raise just for the deposit."

I got up to get the presents I bought for her from Italy while she continued talking.

"I was going to rent but mom said that it was a waste of money. I was even considering going to Joanne's dad to see if he could help me; that is how desperate I am to move out of here. How embarrassing is that to be still living with your mom and dad at twenty-four going twenty-five!" I gave her the present hoping to cheer her up but she just tossed it on her bed and continued so I sat back down on the chair. "After living with Aden and then having to move back home, it's...oh, I don't know; I just feel like my life is moving backward instead of forward. Tracey is married; you are practically married and before I know, Joanne would marry, too. I don't want to end up like my sister, you know; she is going to be thirty-five and she still not married. Every relationship she gets into fails and now look at her, she's moved back home. I guess that was one of the reasons I was so desperate to hang on to my relationship with Aden even though I knew it was not healthy for me. I know he does not love me." I took her hand sympathizing with her but she took it back and continued. "I don't even think he ever did; after all, I was only the consolation prize, right?" She asked tepidly with tears in her eyes.

I got up from the chair I was sitting on to give her a hug but she pulled back not wanting to be comforted.

"You can't save me from this one, Sandra."

As I looked at on my best friend sitting on her bed, I thought to myself that I had never seen her so subjugated. What did Aden do to her? She didn't even wait for me to say anything before she carried on.

"How stupid is this? Can you believe I still love him after all he has done to me? If he came begging to take him back I probably would jump at the chance....but he hasn't even called to see how I am," she turned away from me quickly wiping the tears from her eyes.

I sat back down on the chair and my heart ached for her. I did not realize she felt like that. But then, how could I? I had not been there for her for a long time and she had been going through all that on her own. I lowered my head in shame for being such a bad friend. "Don't feel bad; it's not your fault. I'm a big girl and I chose to see what I wanted to see and besides you tried to warn me about him but I was so caught up in the glitz and glamor and my desire to become a footballer's wife. I ignored all the warning signs. You've always warned me not to be moved by money or be impressed by the people who have them...but I guess it's easy for you because you are rich and now even richer by becoming Gianni Canuti's fiancée."

There was a hint of coldness in her tone. I sensed a bit of resentment from her. I stood up angrily wondering how she could say that to me. I was even more surprised she felt that about me. As I looked down where she sat on the bed, I wondered who she was because this was not the Mandy I knew. She sounded so resentful and bitter; it was as if I was staring at a stranger. I did not realize our friendship had suffered that much. I figured that revealing my true identity was going to crush her the more. I wondered if our friendship had run its course. No! I wasn't going to believe that. I slumped back on the bed with a deep sigh and ran my fingers through my hair not sure where to start from. I prayed inwardly for God to give me the wisdom to know how to handle the situation.

"What about work, are you happy with your work?" I asked.

"If you mean am I a workaholic like you then the answer is no! Other than that, yeah, work is fine," she replied apathetically.

"Amanda Gray, you know I only worked that hard to prove myself and most importantly to forget about Gianni and get him out of my system," I retorted.

"Well, you didn't do a very good job," she replied wittily and we both looked at each other and burst out laughing and embraced ourselves. The laughter turned to cries and apologies.

63

I picked up the bag filled with presents from the bed where she tossed it earlier and handed it to her. She couldn't hold back her surprise. When she opened the first box, she gasped.

"I can't believe it! You bought my ball gown; it is so beautiful," she said quickly opening the rest excitedly.

"You are the best friend ever! You even got me the full accessories; designer matching shoe and handbag. I know I said you were rich but this must have taken you a few modelling jobs and you are not yet Mrs. Canuti." I smiled as she continued, "Even Joanne doesn't spend this much on her own outfit. I feel bad now after saying all that," looking penitent.

"Better to have it in than out....right? Besides, you have been through a lot so I think it's about time we got the old sassy Mandy back," I said pulling her up.

"Come on! Put all these away. I still have a few more surprises up my sleeves. By the time I'm finished, you are going to say 'Aden who?'"

She squealed fervently and rushed to put away her things with great care. I asked her if she wanted her whole family to come to the ball; she hesitated for a while then consented. She ran down to tell them they were excited and even more excited. When I told them I would take care of it, her sister smiled at me. I made a phone call and arranged for outfits for them. Mandy and I went from there to my flat. I opened a bottle of Santiago champagne.

"Are we celebrating something?" she enquired.

"You could say that," I replied.

I got the champagne glasses and poured for us to drink. I handed her a glass then raised mine to make a toast.

"What are we toasting for?" she queried.

"To your new flat," I said taking a sip of my drink motioning her to drink hers. She stared at me with a blank expression.

I walked off to the kitchen leaving her there still staring and obviously baffled.

"You mean you want me to move in here with you?" she asked.

"No!" I replied and her countenance expressed even more confusion.

"I am giving you my flat; call it an early birthday present," I clarified.

"P...p...pardon?" she stammered gob smacked.

I went and got my drink, took a sip and sat down on the sofa.

"You heard me. You can move into the flat on Sunday since we have the ball tomorrow. I won't have the chance to have my things moved until Sunday. Now stop staring at me with your gob opened; you better close it before a fly sneaks in there."

She sat on the sofa still holding her champagne glass. She suddenly drank all of it in one go as the bubbles went up to her nose. I couldn't help but laugh. She put her glass down and threw her arms around me and started to cry.

"This is the happiest day of my life, Sandra. I was wrong when I said you could not save me from all the hurt caused by Aden. I don't know how you do it but you always pull through for me even in an impossible situation. You have always been there for me when it mattered. You are the best friend I could ever wish for. I love you and I am so sorry for being such a cow earlier," she said apologetically.

"Ah, you are just saying that because you have yourself a spanking new flat, Miss Gray," I said frolicsomely pushing her away.

"Yeah, well, there is that, too," she replied and we both laughed.

Still jubilant, we headed for a salon to do our nails. I called my chauffeur this time to drive us. Grandpa had insisted that I'm driven around with a bodyguard at all times. I was reluctant at first but it didn't seem like he was going to concede. On the way, I asked Mandy to know what happened that day for her to end up in the hospital. She hesitated for a moment.

"You know what? I have not been able to talk to anyone about this since it happened but I'm okay to talk about it now," she said taking a deep breath.

"Well, you know how things started in the beginning. Everything was fun and exciting," she smiled and continued, "Wow! I mean Mandy Gray, a nobody, was dating a top football player; even my mom and dad were chuffed. My dad got season tickets to the games; for the first time, my sister was jealous of what I had." I looked at her and was about to tell her how wonderful she was and did not need a footballer in her life to prove she was somebody. "I know what you're going to say, but you have to understand; I'm not like you. Things are different for you; you can get any man you want just by a click of a finger. When Aden showed interest in me, it was like a dream come true. All of a sudden I was important, the newspaper and magazines wanted to take pictures of me. I finally got a taste of what the celebrity life was like.

But it didn't last. Pretty soon I realized that being in the limelight was not all it was cracked up to be. Rumors of Aden with other women began to transpire. When I asked him about it, he would, of course, deny. I caught him in our bed with some prostitute eventually. I was so blown away that I couldn't even say a word. I ran out and tried calling you but I could not get through so I went to my parents' for a few days. He came by and apologized and said she meant nothing to him blah, blah, blah; anyway, we made up.

I went back with him. Not long after, he started to drink heavily and took cocaine with his footballer friends. Whenever we went to some party or a club, he would try to get me to take some cocaine but I would decline. He would mock me saying I was no fun and when he got high, he would become pretty nasty," she paused reflecting.

"He started taking the drugs more and more. I told him he needed to get help and the newspapers were having a field day with him. I'm quite surprised that you didn't read about it. Well.... actually I am not surprised because I know how you throw yourself into your work and don't see anything around you but your work. Anyway, he humiliated me a few times publicly. There were so many public rows about his constant flirting with other women. It got so bad that he would even kiss them in front of me.

I was too ashamed to move back home so I put up with it and hoping he would change. I started drinking heavier than normal. It was like we were living separate lives for a year. It seemed like just the sight of me irritated him. He would taunt me and call me all manner of names. He would call me ugly and ask why I couldn't be more like Sandra. He said that you are the type of woman any man would be proud to be seen with."

I took her hand feeling sad for what she had to endure. She smiled and continued.

"It's okay, I don't feel sad. In fact, hearing myself say it, I can't believe what a jerk he was. Anyway, things reached the fever pitch that Saturday night when after the game, some of his footballer friends came to the house. It was as though I was invisible. I couldn't continue to live like that. When his friends left, I went up, packed my things and told him I was leaving him — this time for good. He pulled my bags from my hands and told me that nobody walked out on him unless he said so. I pushed him and he slapped me across the face very hard I was so taken aback. I just stood there. I was so frightened I took my bags back upstairs. I stayed up there and cried for about an hour until he came in and commanded me to get cleaned up to go back downstairs.

Uncertain what he would do, I went down reluctantly and found him taking more cocaine. He motioned for me to sit next to him. I was scared that if I didn't do what he wanted, he would beat me up. I sat down and watched him as he sniffed the cocaine then he forced me to sniff it. The next thing I knew, I was in hospital fighting for my life."

"Oh Mand," I cried throwing my arms around her.

"Hey!" she said, pulling me off her slowly.

"Enough with the water works; nothing is going to bring me down today. I am far too happy for that so dry your tears. You know I can't stand it when you cry," she said wiping away my tears.

"I feel so much better now that I have told you this. I thought I knew what I wanted; I thought he was going to be my Prince Charming. I really wanted to believe he was the one. Do you know the funny thing? For the first time in a long time, I feel as if a scale has been removed from my eyes and I can see clearly now. I feel so free of Aden. I don't even think I loved him. Maybe I loved the idea of us but then when I look at it, we had nothing in common. I just wasted what? About three years of my life with a guy who was not worth my spit." she said with an upbeat tone.

"That's the spirit," I applauded, "it's good to have the old Mandy back."

When we arrived at the Dorchester Hotel, Mandy looked at me strangely. The driver opened the door for us. The moment we stepped out of the car, the paparazzi outside started snapping pictures crowding around us before I knew it; my bodyguards came and escorted us inside the hotel.

"The perks of becoming the next Mrs. Canuti, huh?" I said before Mandy could ask any questions. She smiled, I didn't want to explain to her the real reason yet.

When we were done with the nails, the spa and had something to eat, we went back to my flat. It was so good to hang out with her and catching up. I really had missed her. Suddenly, she said something that surprised me:

"Now I know there is a God. Anthony was right; there is truly a God who answers our prayers. Do you know what? I am going to give this church thing a go for real this time. It seems to be working for Tracey and Anthony; what do you think?" She asked looking for my approval.

I expressed my thoughts on the matter letting her know how wonderful our God is and how I too definitely was going to start rebuilding my relationship with Him and be serious about church. We embraced, happy and relieved to know how blessed we were;

the two of us were going to give our lives to Jesus. I went and got a card from the table along with my car keys.

I gave her the card for the people who were going to do their hair and make-up in the morning and also the names of the people who were going with the outfits for her family. She could not speak; actually, she didn't have to.

"One more thing," I said taking her right hand and dropping the keys in her palm, "This is for you. My car is now yours; you can drive yourself home."

She burst out crying then hugged me so tight I had to pull away slightly.

"I think you better sit down first to compose yourself before you set off. We don't want anything happening to you or your car before you get to enjoy it, do we?" I cautioned.

It was quite rare to find Mandy speechless so it was interesting to see.

"When you do things, you really go all out; don't you? I left my house this afternoon feeling empty and miserable and here I am going back full and ecstatically joyful and it's all thanks to you," she said with great gratitude still sniffing.

"No!" I replied, "It's all thanks to God, thank Him."

"This is the happiest day of my entire life. I don't think it gets better than this," she said emotionally.

"This is just the beginning," I assured and told her to get going that I still had something to do before bed. She hugged me at the door once again telling me I was the best friend in the whole wide world. We said our good night. I closed the door and called Anthony immediately telling him I was sending his outfit and his parent's ones, too. I also informed him a limo would pick them up.

He just thanked me and said he was going to see me at the ball. I called Tracey to tell her the same thing. I finally got ready for bed after calling grandpa to say goodnight. We spoke briefly and arranged to meet at Dorchester Hotel for breakfast because it was near the house my mom, dad and I used to live. He wanted me to see the house as it had become my house.

I rang Gianni last to say goodnight and to hear his voice even though we had seen each other at work early on. I filled him in on everything that happened and thanked him for making all the arrangements for the outfits and for the limos. I also asked him to meet me at Dorchester after breakfast because I wanted him there with me when I entered that house again. We did not speak too long because Saturday was going to be a very busy and long day. We kissed and said goodnight.

Chapter Six

Welcome Back Home

The breakfast was lovely at the Dorchester but I could not really eat because I was a bit apprehensive about seeing the house. I wondered if I would remember anything about it so I was pretty quiet throughout breakfast. I think grandpa was worried too about how I felt. He kept looking over at me and giving me reassuring smiles. Gianni met us at the lobby and the three of us got into the car and were driven to the house. When we approached the street to the house, it seemed so quiet that it reminded me of the street of Professor Higgins in *My Fair Lady*.

It was a Georgian residence with private garden which connected mews house off Park Lane between Grosvenor Square and Hyde Park. My heart skipped a beat as we got out of the car to behold the magnificent white house. Gianni came and put his arms around me. I looked up at him and smiled bravely. Grandpa asked if I was ready; I nodded in agreement after taking a deep breath. He opened the door and stepped inside. Gianni and I followed behind; I smelled fresh paint. Grandpa said he had just had it painted to freshen up the place as it had been empty since my parents died. Every other thing was more or less as they were then. He handed the keys over to me.

"All yours now, Alexis! Welcome back home," he said with joy.

I walked through the hall hugging myself as if the room was chilly. I headed straight to my parents' bedroom which was a master bedroom with en suite bathroom and separate dressing room. When I opened the door, there was a familiar feeling to it; for a moment, I expected my parents to be there to welcome me back with great joy. I walked in sadly towards the dressing table with a monogrammed chair with the letter "V" engraved on it. I ran my fingers over the chair then pulled it out and sat down.

I looked at the mirror and stared at myself wondering if there was any resemblance to my parents. I picked up the photo frame of the two of them to my right and looked at them and myself. I was not aware when grandpa walked into the room to check on me. He said in passing that I did look like them that I had my dad's eyes but my mom's lips and bone structure. I got up and went over to him and told him I was fine, though, truly, I wasn't. When he suggested taking a tour around the house, I agreed slightly relieved. We took the lift to start from the top to work our way down.

The house had eleven bedrooms and five reception rooms, drawing room, and between the main house and the mews house is the private terraced garden, swimming pools, a big garage to fit about six to seven cars, dining room, a study, kitchen/breakfast room, sauna, gym, laundry room, and two maids' rooms with bathrooms and wine cellar. The house was so much bigger inside than when you look at it from the outside. The house was way too big to be lived in alone and it wasn't going to be long before I would get married, I thought. I loved the marble en suite bathrooms, the elegant curved staircase, and the French-Empire-style grandeur which were great for entertainment.

In a matter of fact, I loved everything about the house. When we got back down, grandpa left Gianni and me alone and went to his room on the second floor. I slumped down on the soft cream sofa, put my feet up on the footstool taking the cushion and hugged it to my chest gazing up at the ceiling and reflecting on the tour of the house. I imagined how joyous it must have been as a family living there. Gianni came round and moved my leg and sat down next to me and asked if I was alright. I looked at him giving him a weak smile.

I asked him if he remembered coming here to play or spend time with me and my family. He said he remembered just a little. I sat up eager to hear what little he remembered but when he saw I was looking a bit sad, he paused and asked if I wanted a drink. I declined. Unsure of what to do, he asked if I wanted my grandpa but I assured him I would be fine. He moved closer and gave me a hug and said,

"You will always have me; my parents are here and your grandpa, too. I pulled back gently from the hug and smiled trying to fight back my tears. "I know it doesn't make up for the loss of your parents but you have a lot of people who love you and would do anything for you," he said trying to reassure me.

I stood up and walked away despondently.

"But nobody lives forever, right?" I asked rhetorically.

"I mean we are here today; gone tomorrow. No one knows when they would die and leave the ones they love behind."

I turned around facing him hoping for something but not knowing what, he looked so sad and depressed. I decided to pull myself together and focus on the ball so I smiled at him.

"You know what? I reckon we should live each day to the fullest starting right now!"

I pulled him up from the sofa and put my arms around him,

"Well, Mr. Canuti, as your soon-to-be wife....what is it you most desire from me once we are married?"

"Ooh," he said smiling and pondering on the question.

"I already have my heart desire right here in my arms; so long as I have you, I have everything."

He kissed me tenderly and told me he could not wait for me to be his wife and if it were possible, he would elope and get married that very day. As we stood for a while, my eye caught the clock on the wall; I needed to head off.

I left grandpa and Gianni at the house as I needed to have a good rest and be ready for the ball. I awoke to the ringing of the phone; I picked up half asleep.

"Wake up, sleeping beauty!" sounded Gianni's voice on the line. "Cinderella must get to the ball on time," he added.

"And who are the ugly sisters?" I jested sitting up.

"That would be Gina and Joanne," he replied.

"Be nice," I said laughing.

"At least, it made you laugh. Now I know you are up," he said. I'll get ready and pick you up at 5:00 pm, Caro bene? Darling okay?"

"Si," I replied.

As soon as he put the phone down, I climbed out of bed and jumped in the shower, washed my hair and started getting ready. Not long after I came out of the shower, my stylist arrived. She did my hair and left. I applied the make-up and slipped on my ball gown. I was putting the finishing touch when Gianni knocked at my door. I walked over to the door in a graceful manner and opened the door

"Wow!" He exclaimed in adoration as he stepped inside and closed the door. He kissed both of my cheeks and gave me a beautiful silk wrist corsage. When I looked at him puzzled, he merely commented that he missed out on giving it to me on our prom so that was a good time as any. I gave him a tender smile and hugged him thinking how romantic he was. I picked up my handbag from the table and we left.

We arrived at the banqueting suite and the place looked lovely and well decorated for the occasion. The team of caterers and other staff were still setting up as we arrived. Ten minutes later, Annabel arrived with her mom. She went over to make sure everything was running smoothly but I told her to relax and enjoy herself.

The ball was due to start at 6 pm but attendees started arriving from 5:35 pm. Gianni and I positioned ourselves at the entrance to welcome the people as they arrived. Mandy and her family came before 6 pm; they looked so wonderful. Anthony and his parents followed. His mom and dad embraced me and thanked me for everything and also congratulated me and Gianni on our upcoming wedding. Anthony went towards Gianni, they greeted politely then he turned to me and smiled broadly.

"You look breathtakingly beautiful," he complimented kissing my cheek with all sincerity and love.

I glanced over at Gianni slightly who shifted uncomfortably tightening his jaws a bit. I knew he was jealous.

"You don't scrub up too bad yourself," I said lightening the mood.

"Women always throw themselves at my son but he is a good boy," said Janet proudly.

"I know...he always was," I replied smiling at Anthony and nodding at some other guests arriving who were greeting Gianni. Once the rest of the Canuti and the Santiago families arrived, the ball officially kicked off.

Joanne came late to the ball, as usual, trying to make an entrance, I guess. Upon her arrival, she came straight to where I was and embraced me, thanking me for inviting her. I took her to where Mandy and her family were sitting. Mandy stood up, greeted her, and the three of us went to Tracey who was sitting down with John on their table. Tracey was a bit surprised to see

Joanne; nevertheless, she understood my reason for coming over. So she got up and followed us out to a quieter place to resolve our differences. Joanne once again apologized to Tracey and asked for forgiveness; Tracey ponders for a moment then smiled accepting her apology. We had a group hug. I instructed them to wait for me there as I went to look for Anthony who had been avoiding me the whole evening.

I spotted him coming back from the gents so I intercepted and asked if I could have a word with him. I led him to where the girls were. Unsure where to begin, a Bible Scripture came to mind.

"Let him who is without sin cast the first stone," I said looking at each and every single one of them but no one said a word; so I continued.

"Look, what has happened has happened. None of us can take it back inasmuch as we may want to. Let's put it behind us and move on. We have all known one another for a long time now and we have shared a lot together. Yes, I know we may not always see eye to eye on some things but we know who we are and have decided to accept one another." Anthony and Joanne looked away so I continued: "Friendship like ours is very rare; I know we are changing and moving in different directions but that does not mean our friendship has to die." Mandy looked at me and smiled. "Do you know that friends do and say the most stupid things to one another but they make up too? When your friendship stands the test of time, that is when you know it is true friendship. I love each and every one of you in your own unique personalities and I thank you for being such good friends to me over the years and more," I said directing my gaze at Anthony lovingly.

I took his hand and Joanne's and joined it together and told them to make peace and forget the past. They edged closer but let go of each other's hand and stood there not knowing who had to go first.

"Forgiveness is the first step to healing and moving forward," I said to encourage them. Then Anthony finally spoke up and apologized and asked her to forgive him but she interrupted and begged for his forgiveness. She admitted she was thoughtless and selfish and wished she could turn back the hand of time. Once the air was cleared, everyone was very chatty and cheerful. Mandy told them what had happened with Aden and we applauded her for her positive steps out of that horrid relationship. Mandy and I told them of our news of giving our life to Christ which shocked them all and was but very pleasing to Anthony and Tracey.

It was like old times again. We walked back to the ball. I excused myself because I had to go and attend to some of our guests so I told them if I didn't speak with them for the rest of the night, we would all meet up for dinner at some point during the week. For the rest of the night, I was pretty much busy as was Gianni. Giovanni came over to me and praised me for the great turn out; that year, our client list increased dramatically. I was so proud of our team; they really deserved a raise for all the effort they put in to the success of the ball.

I went over to the table where our families were sitting and sat next to grandpa. He said he had been watching me all night and he could see how good I was with people and how I would make a great businesswoman; everyone agreed. The music came on and I danced with Gianni's dad, then his grandad, followed by my grandad, and finally I danced with Gianni. I lay my head on his shoulders as we danced; I was beginning to feel really tired. After few more dances, we went and sat down. It was indeed a blissful night.

We all went back to my parents' home; now my new home. It was about 2 am and I was tired. I kicked off my heels and put my feet up while Gianni gave me a foot massage. We sat around for a while then I went up to my room and had a shower, wore one of my mum's clothes that I found in her wardrobe — I didn't even think twice then I went back downstairs. When Gianni came down, we prayed and I asked if it was okay for Gianni to sleep in my room but promised nothing would happen. They agreed so we headed off to bed. It was strange sleeping in my parents' bed but I was too tired to think about it. Gianni and I cuddled up and fell asleep pretty quickly.

When I woke up about midday, the house was not as full; Rosa, Giovanni, and his mom, Carmella, had gone to church. Luciano, Gianni, and grandpa were in the drawing room. I went to my room, showered and changed into one of my mom's clothes again then I came out and was directed by one of my new maids to where everyone was.

After greeting them, I went to eat my food then I went through my parents' personal belongs. I wondered why grandpa never cleared out their things. I figured, perhaps, he just could not face the fact that they were gone. I decided to have a clear out and say a final goodbye to them. I pondered for a moment and unsure how grandpa was going to take it. I had to wait until Rosa returned from church to seek her advice on the matter. I was seriously feeling drained so I laid down on my bed and fell asleep.

It was about 4 pm when I woke to find Gianni sitting on the chair opposite my bed and watching me as I slept. I asked what he was doing. He told me that he wanted to make sure I was okay which I thought was very sweet of him. He said I was tossing and turning in my sleep and whimpering, he considered whether to wake me or not.

I went to have a shower. When I came out, Gianni was still in my room. He asked if I was feeling better. I informed him that I was. I got changed yet into another outfit of my mother's, tied my hair up and just added lip gloss then I called Mandy and asked her to meet me at my flat to collect the keys. She let out a sigh of relief and said she thought I might have changed my mind but knew me better than that.

Gianni and I arrived at my flat by 5:30pm. Mandy got there 30 minutes after. I had packed some of my belongings but I left a lot of my clothes and shoes for her and all the furnishers. She arrived with her whole family; I was a bit surprised but no more so than Gianni. They had never been to my flat before so they were very curious and were really peeking around and vastly eager to have a full look around. It was an atmosphere of mixed feelings: her mom was thankful; her sister was a bit envious of the sudden turnaround and her dad was simply over the moon that his daughter would be living in such a posh area. I handed over the keys to her. She took the keys squealed with delight.

I could see the big expressive smiles on her family's face. They were stunned when I informed Mandy that the rest of the things in the flat were all hers. Her mom started to cry and the dad began to shake Gianni's hand.

"Thank you so much, sir; now I know Sandra is in good hands. I know for sure you will take very good care of her and I hope one day our Mandy will find some as good as you," he expressed in profound gratitude. Then he turned to me and gave me a big hug sniffing as if he was also crying.

He thanked me for being such a good friend to Mandy and the family and for all the help I had rendered over the years. I said my goodbyes to them then Mandy gave me a big squeezed hug which was very emotional then I left with Gianni. We stopped over at his flat for him to pack some of his clothes, too, as he would stay at my place from time to time. Meanwhile, Rosa called. I mentioned to her the idea of finally putting away my parents' things and she assured me that grandpa would not mind at all. She also advised that I stopped work to focus on the wedding preparations which I agreed even though I had made plans to go to work the following day.

Gianni packed practically all his clothes from his wardrobe. When I asked, he laughed and said that home was where I was and that if I was not with him in his flat, then he was going to be with me in my house.

When he was ready, we left. By the time we got back to the mansion, grandpa was back and he was eating with Luciano and

Carmella at the dining table. We joined them to eat. When I was thinking to get grandpa's approval to clear the rooms, he told me that he had gone ahead to have everything boxed up and ready to be sent to charity except for some personal things he thought I would want to keep to remind me of them. I gave him a hug and thanked him feeling lighter within me. That night in my room, I snuggled up to the pillow smiling, thinking about how happy Mandy was and wondered if she would be able to sleep that night. I looked at the clock by my bedside and it was nearly midnight.

I woke up late in the morning so there was a big rush to get to work. Everyone was in high spirit that day talking about the ball and how great a time they had: how some people embarrassed themselves after having too much champagne and the new hook-ups. We had a staff meeting that morning during which talk of a raise and bonuses were brought up which pleased the workers. The rest of the day went pretty fast. I was tired and ready for home by the close of work that day.

Chapter Seven

You are with Child

The euphoria at the office on Tuesday was subsided by Gina's return; missing the ball was not one she was going to take well and, worst of all, her visit to Shanghai was not that needful. I added to her frustration when I played down the report from her visit. Most of all, I ignored her throughout the day. Gianni was preoccupied with the family meeting that was to be held in the evening. I was not really sure what the meeting would be about but I knew it was an important one that may be about Gianni and me. He spent most of the day in his office stressed out. Toward the end of the day, I dashed into his office to ensure that he finished up so we could leave on time. When I entered his office, he lifted up his head from the piles of paperwork on his desk and smiled. He asked if it was time to go; I said yes but we still had five more minutes. He closed the file in his hand and put it on top of the other piles to his left.

The office was pretty quiet now as most of the staff members had left already. His face was so tense and stressed so I walked over to him and sat on his lap giving him a kiss on his forehead to assure him that everything was going to work out and we were going to be married in less than three weeks. Just then, Annabel came in to say goodbye to us.

"Ooh, you're getting married in three weeks, wow! I better start looking for my outfit," she said putting her hand on her mouth excitedly.

"Oh! I am so excited I can't wait; it's going to be the wedding of the year," she added.

"Shhh, we have not yet announced it; keep it down; will you?" I cautioned smiling.

She nodded in agreement and left. A drive home was a somber one as Gianni and I were lost in our own thoughts worried about the family meeting. As we got out of the car, we held hands as if we were about to face a great battle together and entered the house. Both families were already present as we walked in. It was as though they were all waiting for us. Gianni spoke in Italian asking if we were late. Gianni's dad replied that we were not late that rather they were early. We went to freshen up to join the rest for dinner.

When I came back down, everyone was seated at the dining table. Meal time was as lively as usual. We marched to the reception room for the anticipated meeting. The chairs were arranged as though it was a board meeting. Gianni and I sat next to each other. Grandpa, Luciano, and great grandpa, Giovanni, sat side by side at the head table. Before the meeting began, Rosa stood up and insisted that we prayed. Reluctantly, the elders got up followed by the rest. Giovanni Snr. began by stating how happy he was for my return to the family and how God had a purpose for Gianni and me. He paused and looked at everyone and turning to grandpa, he said that the situation we were facing was the same situation his grandmother faced. And the presence of both families was owed to her great sacrifice. I was confused I could not understand what he was talking about but he continued to say that the Santiago family had been placed in the same situation as the Canuti family was in, many, many years ago. Moreover, that it would be very wrong of the Canuti family to expect the Santiago bloodline to come to an end now that a glimpse of hope had smiled at the Santiago family once more.

"No! Sarebbe il male di noi - No! That would be evil of us," he said then sat down.

Luciano speaking after Giovanni Snr. commended his dad for uttering words of wisdom and added that the Canuti family were at the mercy of the Santiago family and whatever decision we came up with, they were going to accept. "No!" came an outburst from Gianni as he stood up and interrupted.

"Son," his dad called out embarrassed by his outburst.

"I cannot lose her again dad, I won't," he groaned. His voice filled with emotions.

"Sit down, Gianni!" His mom instructed. He sat back reluctantly as his grandad continued.

"I know this can't be easy for any of us especially for the two of you," he said fixing his gaze on Gianni and me. I was still puzzled by the whole thing but clearly, Gianni knew what was going on. But what did he mean about losing me again? Why would he lose me? I tried had to focus on what Luciano was saying.

"But we have to make some very tough decisions. We want the wedding between the two of you to take place but not at the expense of ending the Santiago family bloodline," he sat down after speaking.

I glanced over at great grandma hoping she would say something; just anything to make sense of all that but she just patted my hand sympathetically that made me feel worse. I then looked at grandad who was obviously confounded of what to say; he stood up anyways to address us.

He objected to ending the Santiago family bloodline but added.

"My granddaughter's happiness comes first," he looked tenderly at me and smiled. A tear ran down my face as I was beginning to understand what they were talking about. Gianni held my hands as he was relieved by my grandad's words.

Great grandmother spoke advising us to look at the big picture and not with parochial interests. Everyone looked at me expecting that I'd say something but I had nothing to say; I kept my head down processing all that was being said.

There was an awkward silence in the room then Carmella suggested grandpa remarrying to have more children. For a moment there, we looked hopeful but he rejected the idea and said he did not want to marry anyone other than for love and Olivia was his one true love. He also said that the harmony in the family might be jeopardized if the woman does not get along with me and the rest of the family. Most importantly, he did not want any in-fighting among members of the family about the wealth. In a way, we understood; it did not, however, take away the frustration and the sadness that engulfed us especially Gianni.

We went to bed with heaviness in hearts with the matter still unresolved. In the morning, I did not feel like having breakfast so I left in a rush leaving Gianni behind because I did not want to face an uncomfortable drive to work; I was not in the right frame of mind and I had nothing comforting to tell him as I also needed to hear something positive.

I was not in the mood to do anything at work but I noticed Gina kept trying to be super nice to me which I ignored. Annabel had a look of guilt on her face each time she came to my office but I was too preoccupied to find out why; she eventually came to my office and asked if she could have a word with me. She confessed that Gina overheard her on the phone with her mom discussing a new outfit for my wedding. She told me that she was really sorry and didn't mean for it to happen. I told her not to worry about it;

relieved, she left my office.

I looked out of my office window at Gina and thought, "That would explain why she was being so nice to me." I had to be watchful of her. My mind was all over the place as I could not concentrate. I decided to call Anthony. I really needed to talk to him about all what was happening as I could not confide in anyone else but him. As I picked up the phone to call him, Gina walked into my office with a cup of tea and a smile. I put the receiver back down and watched her as she put the tea on my desk and said she thought I needed it as I had not been myself all day. She smiled politely and left. Immediately, Rosa's words came ringing in my ear about Gina trying to poison me; I dared not touch it.

The beverage was later tested and it was indeed poisoned. Gianni wanted to call my grandpa immediately but I told him not to since it would be a bad idea because he would insist on dealing with the matter himself and we knew what that meant. We decided to bring in the police. And when she walked back into my office, I pretended to be feeling poorly. She looked at the mug and saw the cup empty, she gave a broad smile like a Cheshire cat. I acted like I wanted to faint then I reached for the phone and told her I was calling Gianni to come and take me home. She asked to stay with me while he came, I nodded in agreement.

Gianni later came in with the police to Gina's surprise. I shook my head in pity for her and sad that she would not let go of Gianni and how far she was willing to go to get what she wanted. It was really sad to watch as the police officer led her out of my office. She bowed in shame as the office staff raised speculative eyebrows and watched as she was led out of the building. The staff became loquacious with some of them running to Annabel to find out what she knew. Gianni and I went back to my office where I sat down. All of a sudden, the room was hot, quiet, and heavy with languor. He asked if I was okay, but how could I be, I thought. Someone just tried to kill me. I grabbed my handbag and told him I had to get out of the office. When I got home, no one was in which was brilliant because I really did not feel like talking to anyone. I went straight to my room and fell into my bed. I blocked everything out and tried to sleep with a little help with shots of brandy.

The craziest idea came to me; how I came up with that idea the following morning at work, I couldn't tell. But it sounded like the best solution at the time; I was going to have a child who will be adopted by my grandad. When Gianni arrived at the office concerned for my well-being as I had been avoiding everyone, he came straight to my office. I kissed him all excited to run my idea by him hoping he would agree. He loved the idea. We called my grandpa to request the continuation of the previous family meeting. Also, we arranged a staff meeting to inform them of the changes that would take place. It was quite a surreal time. In the staff meeting, Gianni and I informed them about what happened with Gina and what was going to happen with me once I became Mrs. Canuti.

Shortly after the meeting, I went back to my office. Annabel walked in hastily, forlorn and sat down.

"You are leaving tomorrow?" she asked.

I smiled sadly nodding my head.

"But why?" she asked whining. "Now Gina is gone and things are going to be great here and you are going to be Mrs. Canuti. Everything is perfect; why do you want to leave? Please don't leave; what am I going to do when you are gone?"

"Oh Annabel, you are the best secretary ever and whoever takes over from me would be very happy to have you," I said reassuring her.

"I don't think I want to work for anyone else. You are the best boss ever and a good friend," she said almost tearful.

The phone rang interrupting us; I motioned to her that I needed to take the call so she left. It was grandpa; he was ringing to let me know that he had informed everyone and that the meeting was scheduled after dinner. I felt good and was looking forward to lunch with Gianni. It felt like a long time since we had time to ourselves and did normal things together without drama. I drafted a letter for Annabel to inform clients about my leave. I went to get Gianni for lunch.

When we got to Carluccio's Restaurant, the staff was just as I predicted exuberant. After our meal, we drank our champagne leisurely and just enjoyed being in each other's company. The rest of the day went pretty fast for me though not fast enough for Gianni as he was eager about the night.

At home, the meeting began right after dinner. I was fretful at first but grandpa whispered in my ear, "We are all family here, say what is in your mind, Cara."

I stood up, took a deep breath and began.

"Thank you all for coming. I know for the past few days our minds have been troubled about the upcoming marriage."

I paused and continued, "It seems that all the weight of the outcome falls on my shoulders. Before I say what I have to say, I want you all to know I have thought about this very carefully and I did not reach this decision lightly."

Glancing over at Gianni, "I want you to know that I love you very much and I also cannot imagine my life without you."

He smiled at me then I looked at everyone else and continued, "I don't want the Santiago name to end with me. I can't allow the family name to be erased knowing that I could have done something to stop it."

I paused and gave grandpa and great grandma a look for the encouragement which they gave with a warm smile and a nod. I could feel the burning glare from Gianni and I was not quite ready to meet his gaze yet. I looked over at his mom who had her hands to her mouth and his dad with a look of disbelief. His great grandad, grandad, and his grandma were a lot more sympathetic in their expressions. The look of betrayal on Gianni's face was piercing.

"I am just going to get straight to the point. I feel the best and the only solution to this problem is for me to have a son. For Gianni and me to have our first son and give him to grandpa to adopt; that way, everyone wins."

Every eye in the room was transfixed on me as if they could not believe what they had just heard but in Gianni's eyes, it was a look of relief.

"Well," I hesitated, "I will leave you all to think about it unless someone else comes up with a better idea," then I sat down.

There was silence in the room for a moment as everyone pondered on what I had said. I stood up again clearing my throat, I turned to the Canuti's.

"There is an alternative if you will find it difficult to give up the child to become a Santiago. We can postpone the wedding and have the child fathered by artificial insemination by someone I trust and can totally rely on plus he won't mind doing this for me…."

Before I could finish, Gianni stood up indignant by the suggestion.

"Oh! Now I understand, someone you can trust and rely on, someone who won't mind doing this for you after all…he is Mr Perfect, Mr wonderful; Dr. Anthony. Oh! I bet he wouldn't mind doing it since he struck out in marrying you. I'm sure he would only be too happy to father your child. Why don't you just admit you are still in love with him; that's what all this is about, right?" He said vindictively.

I slapped him really hard across the face as I was hurt by his careless comment.

"Do you think I want this? Do you think I want to be put in this position?" I yelled back, "Can you just think about anyone else besides yourself for once. Marriage is about compromise and from the sound of things, I don't think you are ready for it."

I apologized to the rest of the family and excused myself. I headed toward the door.

"Yeah that's right, run back to him like you always do when things get tough," he yelled.

I looked over at him bitterly and he had no look of remorse, the others looked on in horror. I screamed and slammed the door in aggression. I took the keys to his car and drove straight to Anthony's.

He was not in when I got there so I let myself in with my old keys. I fell on the sofa and slept. I was not asleep for long before Anthony woke me up shocked to see me in his flat. With great concern, he immediately asked if everything was okay. I apologized to him for letting myself in and told him that it wasn't right for me to hold on to his key. He joked and said not after the Joanne fiasco. He took a closer look at me noticing how pale and tired I looked. Concerned, he insisted on giving me a check-up. I teased him and asked him whether he wanted to give a full body check-up. He laughed and told me to behave myself that he was being serious. I told him to sit down that I had something to tell him. He looked disturbed but I assured him it was nothing for him to worry about.

I took a deep breath, not really sure where to begin as there was so much that had happened in such a short space of time. I began from finding my real family to Gina's attempt on my life and so on. When I finally finished, he stood up bewildered by all that he had heard and rubbed his head. He went to the kitchen and got a glass of water. Just then, my grandpa called; we spoke in Italian as best I could. He wanted to know whether I was okay.

"So you're Italian, huh? Not just Italian but an Italian mafia marrying into another mafia family....boy!" Anthony exclaimed. I punched his shoulder playfully.

"I am no longer living at my old place. I gave my car and apartment to Mandy as she was desperate to move out of her parents'," I said.

"I wanted to cheer her up because of all she had gone through. My new place is in Mayfair; that is, where I was born. I would like you to come for dinner so I can introduce you to my family. I want you and Gianni to get along."

Although bewildered by all that I revealed to him, he understood. I left his place feeling much better and happy.

I got home just after 1:30 a.m. Everyone seemed to be in bed but I could see light in grandpa's bedroom. He came out as I was about to go up to my room to check if I was truly okay as I had claimed on the phone. I assured him I was truly fine so he mentioned that Gianni was not in a very good mood and the manner that I left got everyone worried. He encouraged me to talk to Gianni so we could sort things out. He kissed my forehead then went back to bed. I walked past Gianni's room to see if he was asleep but the light to his room was off so I headed straight to my bedroom. When I put on the light, he was lying on my bed pretending to be asleep. I closed the door putting my handbag on the dressing table.

"I know you are not sleeping," I said, walking towards the bed. He rolled over to face me.

"You know me too well," he replied sitting up.

"Where have you been?"

"Anthony's," I answered.

"Of course," he said in a low sad voice shifting to the edge of the bed.

I sat down at the dressing table and began to remove my make-up as he watched me through the mirror silently in fear of saying the wrong thing. Occasionally, I would return his gaze with both of us wanting to say so much to each other but not knowing where to start from. I finished removing my make-up and got up to go to the bathroom.

"I am going to shower," I said.

"It's nearly two in the morning!" He exclaimed.

I ignored him and went to the bathroom. As I brushed my teeth, I paused for a moment and looked at myself briefly in the bathroom mirror hating all the tension between us and wishing for it to pass quickly. When I came out after my shower, he was still sitting on the bed waiting for me.

"Do you still want to marry me?" He asked.

"Do you?" I threw the question back to him.

"You know the answer to that," he replied.

"Then you know the answer to mine," I said.

He pulled me closer to him telling me how sorry he was for all the things he had said. I apologized for slapping his face as I rubbed the side that I slapped.

"Oh! I will live," he replied.

I kissed it and gave him a big hug, both of us letting out a sigh of relief.

"We really have to talk," I said.

He looked down, "I know," he replied.

"I don't want Anthony to be an issue in our marriage," I said looking into his eyes, "Anthony and I are just friends, good friends and always will be; nothing more."

"I know you two have a strong connection and I don't want you to end your friendship because of my insecurities. It's something I have to deal with myself; I am sorry," he said stroking my face tenderly.

"I know that you are not in love with him and I know with all my heart that you love me. I mean you are willing to give up your child just to be with me; what greater sacrifice could a man ask for? I just get so jealous sometimes about your closeness with Anthony. I can't seem to think clearly."

I explained to him that Anthony was like a brother to me. I proceeded to let him know that Anthony used to be jealous and had every right to because I didn't end up with him after years of waiting for me to become his wife. As if that was not enough, he then found out in the news report I was engaged to marry someone else. I asked him to put himself in Anthony's shoes for a moment. He was silent as if mulling over what I had just said. He left to sleep. I'm sure he spent the whole night brooding on what I told him.

Being my last day at work, I wanted to be at the office early. It felt strange being my last day. I spent the day going through the emails of gratitude from clients, the cards, and the bouquet of flowers; I lost track of time. Gianni came straight to my office glancing at the wall clock.

"Thirty more minutes to go and that's it," he said.

I followed his gaze to the big black and white clock on the wall and smiled getting up to kiss him but I swayed losing my balance and fainted. The next thing I knew, I was in the hospital. After a full check-up, the doctor announced to both of us that I was pregnant. I couldn't remember very well my initial reactions but I was at the same time shocked, happy and concerned. I had mixed emotions but Gianni was just beaming and grinning with excitement. As soon as the doctor left my room, he darted towards me with arms opened wide and gave me a big hug exclaiming his joy. Just then the door opened. It was his parents and my grandad looking concerned. Gianni leaped out of my hospital bed as his mom shut the door and said with great enthusiasm, "Papa, Mama; we are having a baby," throwing his arms on all three of them.

I raised my eyebrows for his lack of self-control as I watched them surprised. There was a loud cheer and happiness all round as they altogether came to my bedside and congratulated me. Each and every one of us chatted happily until the doctor entered then I inquired if I could go home. To my delight, he said yes that I needed to take better care of myself and eat properly and also stay away from stress.

"She will," they all responded in one accord.

That evening, the whole family went out to dinner to celebrate. Everyone was over the moon about the news. I don't think I had ever seen Gianni that happy. During dinner, as everyone chatted blissfully, I leaned over to Gianni and whispered in his ear, "You do realize if this baby is a boy, it is not ours just as we agreed, right?" worried he might have forgotten.

"The more reason why I am happy is because I know it will be a boy," he said.

"And we can now get on with our lives quicker and hustle-free also," he smiled audaciously, "It means the sex ban is lifted."

I told him he had one track mind and we giggled like a couple of schoolkids.

As we got back, grandpa informed us that he would fly back to New York with Luciano and his wife and that my great grandparents were returning to Italy. He explained he had some business to attend to and when he was back, we would release to the press about me being a Santiago.

After a while, I went to my bedroom, dressed down and got in bed. Gianni tucked me in and said goodnight to my surprise. As he approached the door to leave, I cleared my throat to get his attention. He turned around and came back to my bed to find out what I wanted and if I was okay. I pulled him down to sit on the bed then I asked him if he was alright because it was not like him to just tuck me in like a good little girl and walk away without insisting he slept in my bedroom.

"First of all, you really need to rest tonight and, secondly, we will have the house to ourselves from tomorrow so I can wait one night," he smiled and kissed me goodnight again then left; not long after that, I fell asleep.

Chapter Eight

Friends at Last

Saturday morning started off with Gianni bringing me breakfast in bed; it was lovely. By the time I showered, got ready and came down, it was about midday and the house was so quiet. I was so used to having everyone around the house that it felt so empty; I was missing them already. Gianni came behind me putting his arms around my waist and kissing my neck.

"You smell good," he complimented.

I turned and kissed him thanking him for my breakfast. He asked if I wanted to do anything before the designer of the wedding costume came; I thought it was the perfect moment to tell him about my past. I took his hand and led him to sit down where I explained to him that it was the right time to get everything out in the open and start afresh. His facial expression switched and became serious; I stroke his face assuring him that I loved him.

I began with Grandma Faye and how she found me wandering the streets covered in blood all through to when Anthony saved me from the hands of Mr. Abbott's rape attempt.

"The rest you know about," I said as his eyes were filled with tears.

He stood up unable to speak as he paced about with his head bowed. I walked up to him and placed my hand on his shoulder; I rubbed it to let him know that it was fine but all he could do was hold me and wept like a child. I knew he was emotional but I didn't expect him to take it that badly. He went to the bathroom and was there a little longer than normal. He came back, realizing I was worried, explained that he just needed to reflect on everything and re-examine himself.

I poured him a drink and told him I did not mean to upset him and that I wanted him to know everything about me so we could have a better understanding of our relationship. Most importantly, I wanted him to understand my friendship with Anthony. He bade me to stop and asked if I could get Anthony to the house. I didn't know how that could be as Anthony's shifts changed every time. I called all the same. Anthony said he was covering for someone but agreed to come after work. I gave him the address to my new home.

Later in the day, the doorbell rang and the maid opened the door. I stood up slightly worried as Gianni refused to tell me why he wanted to see Anthony and met him in the hallway. Anthony peered in nervously. I smiled and encouraged him that he had nothing to worry about. He looked around admiring the place.

"This place is like Buckingham Palace!" He exclaimed.

I laughed at his slight exaggeration as we walked towards the sitting room where Gianni was waiting. He was standing by the fireplace when we walked in. Anthony was surprised to see Gianni there; he stopped at the doorway no longer sure what was going on. Gianni walked towards us and shook Anthony's hand warmly and thanked him for coming at such a short notice explaining that it was at his request. Anthony glanced at me taken aback as that was the last thing he was expecting to hear from him.

Gianni offered him a drink which he refused; then he motioned for him to sit down. Anthony walked over slowly to the settee and sat down as I went and sat next to Gianni also curious as to what he had to say. Gianni apologized to Anthony for any hostile attitude he may have displayed toward him over the years. He disclosed that for the first time in years, he was able to see clearer and appreciate the kind and wonderful person Anthony was and the amazing friend he had been to me. Anthony shifted uncomfortably in his seat wondering where all that was going as he looked at me for answers. I pretended not to notice.

Gianni stood up and walked towards Anthony who kept a tight gaze at him. I could tell what was going through his mind that precise moment, of course, because I knew he loved watching mafia movies. I smiled at him to reassure him that everything was fine but he was not at all relaxed. Gianni came behind him and patted him on his left shoulder which made him jumpy.

"You are the kind of person that anyone would be proud to call a friend. You are loyal, patient and very understanding. I saw the way you reacted to the ball even when your parents embarrassed you in front of us; I was really impressed and the way you gracefully accepted my engagement with Sandra even though you love her," he said commending him.

Anthony tried to object but Gianni continued cutting him off.

"I know Sandra loves you too and for the bond and closeness you have, only a fool would attempt to break it. Sandra's happiness is my happiness and getting to know you better is important to her so I am willing if you are."

Anthony was enthralled and dumbfounded by what Gianni said; I could not hide my overwhelming joy for such a huge gesture from Gianni. I looked at him in loving admiration. Anthony noticing my joy agreed; they shook hands. We conversed for a while and he became a lot more relaxed. We informed him about our upcoming wedding in a couple of weeks which took him by surprise. A short while later, the doorbell rang; it was the designer. I left the two of them to it and went with the designer to one of the other rooms.

Deciding which dress I wanted took longer than I thought. With the short notice, the designer started feeling the pressure already and she had not even started yet. I dismissed her as I was not at all pleased with her attitude. I called Rosa to give her the disappointing news; she freaked out but I wanted to be comfortable with the person designing my wedding dress. When I went back to the sitting room, I noticed that the boys were not there. The maid informed me their whereabout so I joined them in the pool room.

They were like bosom buddies to my delight. I told them how I dismissed the designer over her poor attitude but did not seem so concerned with that matter and continued playing pool. Men, I thought. They just did not understand so I left them to it and went back to the sitting room. Not long after, Rosa called to inform me she was sending someone else and they would be with me shortly. Whilst I was waiting for the new designer, I was flicking through the bridal magazine when Gianni and Anthony returned to the sitting room. Anthony told me that Gianni had given him a tour of the mansion and he did not realize just how huge the house was. Then Gianni told me that he had sorted out his best man issue which got me thinking that I had not yet let the girls about the date of my wedding. I started dialing Mandy's number.

"Don't you want to know who it is?"

"Sure," I replied, more concerned about sorting out my bridesmaids as Mandy's phone began to ring.

"You're looking at him," he said. Noticing my confusion, he declared, "Anthony!"

I cut the call abruptly not quite sure if I heard him correctly. I looked at him, then I glanced at Anthony who was nodding his head in agreement. I was speechless but before I could utter a word,

Mandy called back. I told her to get the girls to come over to my place. I made sure she was aware that it was a matter of urgency as I needed help with my wedding dress and they needed to sort out their bridesmaids' outfit.

After I got off the phone, I told Anthony and Gianni that it was a wonderful idea but I had a crisis on my hand and if I didn't sort out my wedding dress, there was going to be no wedding. They both shared a look implying I was being overly dramatic. I gave them a disapproving look in frustration and stormed out like a child. I could hear them sniggering. I turned around glaring at them; they quickly camouflaged a serious look. As I continued to walk off, they started laughing.

Thirty minutes later, the new designer arrived and to my surprise and delight, it was Elle from Fame Star designs. I was so relieved I gave her a big hug almost teary. I loved what she was wearing which was a black two tone knitted dress with V-neck, skinny straps, buttons to back, small ribbon to the front and sheer puff sleeves which fitted her petite frame nicely. As always, she was very professional and friendly and knowing the tight schedule, she got straight to work refusing the drink I offered her.

I started to get really stressed as I was caught in a dilemma choosing the best outfit out of a plethora of equally good designs. We ended up with a sketch of the design. She sketched as I described it to her. We then looked at a number of suiting fabrics. We were almost finished when the girls arrived. Gianni and Anthony brought them to me. Mandy's mouth was still left ajar as her eyes circled the room.

"This place is like a palace," she declared.

"You're not wrong there," Tracey confirmed.

"I must say this place is impressive, Gianni," complimented Joanne to Gianni thinking it was his place.

Anthony quickly corrected her and stated it was my place but Gianni and I gave him a look to keep quiet. The girls were all over me about the house. I cut them off and stressed that there was something of a greater importance than the mansion. At that, Gianni and Anthony dashed out leaving us to it.

The girls looked at me inquisitively as I introduced Elle to them. Indubitably to no one's surprise, Joanne recognized her immediately. She asked if Elle was going to design my wedding dress. I nodded and informed them that she needed to take their measurements as they were going to be my bridesmaids with Mandy as maid of honor. They squealed in exhilaration.

"Well, what are we waiting for? Let's get started," Mandy suggested.

It was quite late when we were done; I was famished. I walked Elle to the door as the girls went to the sitting room where Anthony and Gianni were watching football. I joined them declaring how hungry I was. Gianni alerted the chef as we marched to the dining room. We talked enthusiastically about the wedding. The food was served and whiles we ate, the girls continued to come up with ideas for the hen-night but we couldn't agree to a suitable one as I didn't really want a boozy one or a striper to Gianni's delight. I also told the girls that Gianni's mom, Rosa, and grandmother, Carmella, would probably want to join us so we needed to think of something suitable for everyone. I was curious to know what Gianni and Anthony planned on doing for his stag night.

"It's a surprise," they replied simultaneously.

"Another word, you have no idea either," I said doubting. They shook their heads causing the girls to laugh.

They noticed I was not drinking which was very unusual. Gianni and I shared a look and smiled warmly.

"You are pregnant," guessed Tracy.

"That would explain why you looked tired and pale the other night," Anthony recalled.

The girls got up and gave me a hug. Anthony shook Gianni's hand and congratulated us. Once everyone calmed down, I decided to hit them with the final piece of news about who my grandad was.

"In the next few days or so there will be a press release from my grandfather declaring he has found his missing granddaughter and I did not want you guys to find out that way," I said as they listened in suspense wanting me to go on.

"My real name is Alexandra Santiago."

There was silence in the room as they pondered on the name wondering who it could be; then Tracey said she could not think of any famous celebrity called "Santiago."

"The only Santiago I know is the firm I work for," said Mandy.

"Yeah, and the only Santiago I know is my dad's boss who terrifies him anytime he called and, believe me, it takes a lot to scare my dad. I am quite knowledgeable when it comes to celebrities and I am not familiar with any actor or actress with that name," Joanne added.

"Her grandad is far greater than any actor or actress, Joanne. You are looking at the heiress to "The Santiago Empire;" the big Italian mob, the richest Italian family in the world," declared Anthony proudly and all their jaws dropped; they were speechless.

"The owner of my law firm is the late Angelo Santiago, any relations?" Asked Mandy holding her breath hoping I would say no.

"He was my dad," I told her. Joanne stood up hastily and walked over to us questioning if his dad's boss was any relations of mine. I confirmed that, too. She looked at me in horror then took a big gulp of her champagne and went and sat down. Anthony went to the dining table to get some more drinks.

"Wow, impressive! You also make fine champagne too," he said a little louder than normal noticing my surname on the bottle.

"From the sound of things, they seem to own everything," murmured Joanne.

"Now, now, Joanne; no need for jealousy. It's not like you

were any match for her...you've always played second fiddle to her anyway so you should be used to it by now," said Anthony flippantly draining his glass.

"Anthony!" Tracey called sternly appalled by his remark.

"What?!" he questioned, "I am only saying what you are all thinking?"

He walked over to the table and poured more drink for himself as Tracey gave him a disapproving look which he ignored, and Gianni and I started laughing. Mandy walked off and headed towards the sitting room. Gianni motioned with his head for me to go after her.

Mandy's reaction surprised me; but for Joanne's, I didn't expect anything less. I asked her if she was okay and she nodded so I sat down waiting for her to talk but she just stood there.

"So much for my happy news," I muttered.

She looked at me then sat down feeling a bit guilty.

"I am sorry," she said, "So many changes in such a short time. You're getting married and you are now this super rich mafia woman from the most powerful family in the world. It's like I don't know you anymore," she paused, then sat next to me and continued: "It's like I am losing you. I know it sounds stupid but I feel like I am being left behind," she looked at me expecting me to understand but I didn't.

"Yeah, you are right; it does sound stupid," I said upset by her comments.

"Do you know I have never really noticed how selfish you were until now? I mean you work for a top law firm in the city that gave you a training contract when you finished your bar exams, you have a top luxurious flat and a beautiful sports car not to mention the good friends and family who love you but it is never enough; is it? You always want more."

I stood up walking back to the dining room fuming. By the expression on everyone's face, they heard everything.

"This is supposed to be one of the happiest times of my life. I wanted to share it with my best friends but I could see that was a big

102

mistake as my so-called friends are not happy for me," I grumbled turning back to look at Mandy who was behind me, followed by a glare at Joanne.

"Do you know what? I couldn't care less," I walked off in a huff leaving them all as they watched me in amazement. I went up to my room and threw myself on my bed face down feeling dejected. I felt a lump in my throat but I tried hard not to cry until Gianni came in and threw his arms around me then I just broke down and cried.

He held me tighter as he stroked my hair without uttering a word. Fifteen minutes later, we went back downstairs. It was as though everyone there was waiting on tenterhooks in the sitting room. My taciturn friends refused to speak as they were afraid of saying the wrong thing. I went and sat down on the sofa near the television. I noticed Tracey and Joanne nudge Mandy to come over to me and say something. Hesitantly, she moved closer to me and sat at the edge of the sofa. I ignored her and kept my eyes firmly on the television set, not that I cared about what was on. Seeing how much she upset me, she squatted down in front of me and tilted her head to get my attention I but refused to meet her eyes.

"I hope you won't send the mobs after me," she said and smiled apologetically. I glared at her but was not able to hold it and smiled. Joanne and Tracey both joined Mandy apologizing. I smiled as I patted Joanne on the shoulder and gave Tracey a squeeze in her hand as I smiled warmly.

They got up and went and sat back down while Mandy stayed. She asked me if she was forgiven. I just looked at her and thought I couldn't stay angry with her forever and my wedding was around the corner so I asked her whether she had thought of what we were doing for my hen night. Smiling broadly, she leaped forward and gave me a big hug and a kiss on the cheek. I was still a little bit upset but I covered it up smiling as she chatted about the hen night. We joined Tracey and Joanne while Gianni and Anthony came back with some drinks for us. I asked them if they had sorted out the stag night and they shook their heads. I suggested to the girls we flew to Italy or France for the hen night and everyone loved the idea and the guys looked inspired.

"Well, if the girls are flying off to Europe, we can do the same, right?" Gianni suggested to Anthony who was chuffed.

By the end of the evening, everyone was jolly. Anthony was a little tiddly so our driver had to take him home whiles we had his car dropped off at his house. When everyone was gone, I felt drained. All I wanted was to be cuddled up to Gianni and sleep.

The week appeared to have gone pretty quickly. I spent most of it with Rosa sorting out the wedding preparations. Every so often I missed being at work but I was preoccupied with wedding plans. I went to check how my wedding dress was coming along and before I knew it, Friday was upon us. Gianni decided to go to Spain with the private jet while I chose to take my yacht to Monaco. Grandpa and Luciano came back from New York.

All week, the girls called me each day to talk about our weekend away. I kept the yacht part of the package from them as a surprise. We had to leave earlier than the men as they were flying. I sent a car to pick up the girls and bring them to my house. Rosa, Carmela and I met them outside my house as they pulled up. I made a brief introduction then we got into the limo to take us to my yacht. The whole weekend was great. I loved being out with the girls again and I was quite surprised Rosa, my soon-to-be mother-in-law was a great laugh as was Carmela for an old woman. The hen night was unforgettable. Even though I was not drinking, I had a great time.

It went so fast I couldn't believe we were already back to London. The cars were waiting outside for us as the girls and I hugged and kissed goodbye. The guys were already home when we got there. Gianni was really happy to see me as were his dad and grandad. We exchanged stories of our weekend apart and laughed a lot as we revealed the things we got up to. We stayed up until I became very tired and went to bed.

Chapter Nine

Waiting in Anxiety

I couldn't believe I was getting married that weekend. It felt so unreal. Gianni's mom was jitterier than I was. The whole week was full of activities and preparations; so many emails and phone calls. Though, in all honesty, Rosa and Carmela made sure I didn't lift a finger to do anything unless I absolutely had to. It was such a big day; in the evening at six o'clock, grandpa and I would receive the press at the house to announce the return of the long-lost granddaughter of Giuseppe Santiago after all those years.

I was so nervous I wasn't sure if it was because of that or trying on my wedding dress hoping I would look great because I wanted to look perfect for Gianni. Just thinking about it was stressing me out.

It's funny how things could change so quickly. When the designer brought out my dress, everyone's face lit up, especially mine. I admired my dress lovingly almost afraid to touch it as if it was fragile. I walked over to where my dress was hanging and stroked it gently. Tracey urged in anticipation for me to try it on. I looked around at everyone with excitement bubbling inside me. I then took the dress to try it on with the help of the designer. Once the dress was on, I turned around to face everybody who waited patiently.

"You look beautiful; just beautiful dear; your mom would be so proud," Rosa complimented.

I smiled and thanked her feeling closer to her than ever. The rest of them complimented on how beautiful the dress was which pleased the designer a great deal. The assistant handed the maidens' dresses. They tried it on as well and they looked stunning. We posed in front of the mirror admiring ourselves picturing the big day. Rosa and Carmella smiled happily.

"I think we are now ready for the big day," they said relieved.

We changed and went back downstairs with gladness of heart chattering away. The designer and her assistant left shortly after. Grandpa and Luciano got to know the girls better, too.

"Your grandpa is not as scary as I thought," Joanne whispered in my ears. I laughed.

The butler came round with some refreshments for everyone and told grandpa that the press were arriving soon. Grandpa hired more house staff for me insisting that I should not strain myself especially as I was pregnant. So my house was fully staffed with servants and bodyguards. We went to change and by the time I came back down, the press were in the living room waiting for me. After a formal introduction, they set up in the reception. Grandpa spoke first as he read out his statement. Mandy nudged me and Tracey smiled excitedly as she had never been around the press before.

"I introduce to you my long-lost grand-daughter, Alexandra Santiago;" known to you as Sandra Appleton," grandpa declared stretching his hand toward me and beckoning for me to come forward.

I went to stand next to him as they watched stunned by the revelation. Almost immediately, there was a mad frenzy; the cameras flashed frantically in front us and the questions came thick and fast. Grandpa motioned for silence.

"That would be all," he declared to their dismay. They thanked him, however, then the press was dismissed. I was now officially recognized as Alexandra Santiago by the world; the heiress to the Santiago Empire.

Chapter Ten

You May Kiss the Bride

"Tomorrow is the day!" Grandpa declared as I walked down the stairs. "Are you ready?"

"I was born ready," I replied smiling.

The doorbell rang; it was Anthony. He walked in all frazzled. He told us that his parents woke him up the first thing that morning going on about him and me in the news.

"When I came out, some reporters were waiting on my doorstep asking all kinds of questions, and I come here to find tons camped outside your house," he said breathlessly.

"Where is your luggage?" I asked him trying to take his mind off it.

"Oh! The driver said to leave it in the car as we would be leaving shortly," he replied.

One of the servants poured him a cup of tea as we sat down.

The doorbell rang again and it was the girls. They found the whole thing exceedingly exciting. Once everyone arrived, we proceeded to leave. While Anthony and the girls used the front door, Gianni and I used the private exit to the garage. Anthony and Joanne were the decoys for Gianni and me.

Once on the plane, the girls were equally as impressed with the jet as they were with the yacht. We had breakfast on the plane. Inn no time, we landed in Italy. There was a stretch of cars waiting for us on the airstrip upon arrival. They took us to the Santiago Estate where we were received warmly. The Canuti drivers took Anthony and the Canuti's to their house. We agreed to meet at the church at noon.

Great grandma came out to meet us outside the house; I ran to give her a big hug. I spoke to her in Italian which seemed to impress my friends. I introduced them to her and she gave them a kiss on both cheeks greeting them in Italian. They were blown away by the sheer luxury of the mansion. Grandpa commanded the servants to take very good care of the girls and showed them to their rooms. I stayed down to spend some time with my great-grandmother who was very happy to have that time with me. She tried to speak slower so I could understand her but I told her it was not necessary because I had taken private lessons to improve on my Italian. She was thrilled to hear me speaking almost as fluent as her; Grandpa was as well surprised as he was not aware I was taking lessons. She gave me a bear hug laughing aloud.

"Si è oro puro – you are pure gold," she said and grandpa nodded his head in agreement.

She rubbed my tummy and became tearful. When she saw the look of concern on my face, she told me not to be worried for they were tears of joy and not of sadness because she did not think she would live to see her son smile again not to talk of seeing me alive and now a new blood to carry on the Santiago legacy and bloodline. She said that if she were to die, she would die a happy and fulfilled old woman.

I thought the church was magnificent when we got there. When I set my eyes on the building, I fell in love with it. It was lovely and the cathedral was impressively large. The huge building was made of brick faced with marble. Inside, the first thing you notice were the gilded of mosaics that covered the walls and ceilings, the intricately-patterned floor was a 12th-Century mixture of mosaic and marble in geometric patterns. The church was just stunning and I could not have picked a better place to get wedded.

The priest greeted us warmly and introduced himself as Father Severino; he was about fifty years old. He had dark black thick hair with a trace of silver by the side and hazel eyes; he was a good-looking man. He seemed to know our families very well. Strangely enough, he gave me a hug as if I was his long lost relative. I glanced over at Gianni who shrugged his shoulders. Also in the church was the famous wedding planner, Gino Rossetti. The other members of the bridal party were already waiting inside. The flower girl was so pretty with her curly black hair and the page boy was very cute, too. Rosa later informed me that they were distant cousins. After the initial introduction, we quickly got on with the rehearsals.

Gino was every bit eccentric as I had heard and very controlling but he knew what he was doing. I was really impressed; everyone knew what to do and when to do it especially the locals. Gino definitely ran a tight ship; at some point, it felt like I was in a military camp. We went over the whole event and protocol of the day then Father Severino told us to expect the unexpected. I did not like that comment so I asked him what he meant by that. He simply replied that a wedding day had a mind of its own at times but the most important thing was to enjoy the day and remember our vows.

We spent what appeared like hours in the church. By the time we got back to the Canuti estate, it was late afternoon. Gianni and I decided to take Anthony and the girls to see a little bit of the town briefly. Anthony acknowledged his renewed love for Italy and commented that he had been to Italy before but he did not remember it being that beautiful. I did not even know Anthony had been to Italy before, funny that I wonder what else I did not know about. As for Tracey, it became her favorite place in the world then Mandy recalled how she said the same thing about Monte Carlo; we burst out laughing. Joanne, of course, was no stranger to Italy. When we got back, the meal was set in the dining table.

After dinner, we went for a walk in the garden, Gianni and I strolled hand in hand as the others walked ahead of us. When we found a secluded spot, we stopped and sat down. I leaned my head against his shoulder remembering the last time we were there watching the sunset. It was a lovely warm evening and everything looked so perfect. We just sat there in silence basking in the ambiance. I thought of how much I loved the place and everyone in the family then I thanked God for blessing me so abundantly.

I reflected briefly how far I had come then smiled snuggling closer to Gianni; we sat there for what seemed like hours. Gianni kissed my head when we spotted the others coming and said we had to go. I grumbled as I wanted to stay some more because I knew we were spending the night in separate houses. I asked him how he felt about that and he said his consolation was knowing that after the next day, we would be together forever never to be apart again; that thought also comforted me and we got up and joined the others and headed back to the main house.

The driver took us back. Rosa left with us as she was spending the night at mine to ensure I went to bed on time, so she said; but I think it's because she knew as my mum was not there she had to be there to fill that void on such a special occasion — I loved her even more for her thoughtfulness. All I could do that moment was give her a hug. Gino and all my wedding attendants were all staying at my place including my grandmother, Olivia's sisters, brothers and their family members. The mansion was full of people from the main house to the guest house. The compound was packed and more people were still arriving.

Grandpa introduced me to everyone when we got back. There were such joy and gladness in the air; wedding times have a way of bringing loved ones together. I didn't realize I had such a large family and, indeed, everyone was talking about the news report which seemed to be on every news channel. I wondered what the day ahead would be like with the press and tabloids. I could not spend much time with my relatives because I had to go and get my manicure and pedicure done; Tracey and Mandy too but Joanne was ahead of us on that one; her nails were always immaculate. Gino came in whiles we were still chattering after we had had our nails done.

"Okay, Miss Alexis and your attendants, it is now time for bed. You have an early start in the morning," he commanded.

I did not bother to argue with him though it was not that late but from what I had seen of Gino, you could never win an argument against him; it was more peaceful to just comply. We hugged excitedly and went to our rooms.

I woke up at 5:30 a.m. filled with excitement. I went down to get a cup of tea still in my nightgown and silk creamy long robe. I was rather presumptuous thinking everyone was asleep but Rosa was up with some others. She said she could not sleep any longer as she was far too excited to sleep. Rosa insisted on making my tea as it was my day and I was not to lift a finger to do anything. Of course, the maids could have brought us the tea but I think we wanted to do it ourselves to push back the nerves inside us. I sat back down and smiled thanking her. It was lovely to have that moment with an amazing mother-in-law. I watched her make the tea for both of us. We did not talk much; we just enjoyed being in each other's company.

Mandy joined me in my room as soon as I entered. She sat down in her Chanel dark blue short dress and black slippers with a big grin on her face. She jumped up and squealed like a child on a

Christmas morning who could not wait to open their presents and gave me a squeezed cuddle.

"Ooh, you must be so excited," she exclaimed.

Up until that moment, I was fine but I started getting butterflies in my stomach. She told me that Gino demanded that we went down for breakfast then do our hair and make-up as we were on a tight schedule. I had my wedding lingerie laid out on the bed which caught Mandy's eye. She could not resist admiring and teasing me about them. It was a beautiful, soft, seashell ivory silk decorated with tiny multicolored crystals. The Basque had detachable shoulder and suspender straps made from soft blue and pink lace inset with sparkle sequins. It was a lively scene when we went downstairs. However, we could not enjoy enough of it. According to Gino, we had only 15 minutes to finish breakfast. And true to his word, he marched us straight to the styling room.

After the stylist finished our hair, the makeup artist began to work on me immediately. I loved the high bun hairstyle he did on me — it was very elegant. It was like getting ready for a modelling show. By ten o'clock, everyone's hair and make-up were done. I went to my room while the girls and Rosa went to get ready. They really did a splendid job on my hair and make-up that I could not believe my eyes as I sat in front of the mirror.

I wished my parents were there. My mom would be wearing the biggest grin on her face and my dad would be so overly proud walking me down the aisle; I could not resist the sadness that engulfed me. Grandpa's knock jolted me out of it. He looked so handsome in his Brioni suit, custom-made with merino wool. I loved his silk tie as well. My eyes went straight to the box he had in his hand which he held forward as he approached. I got up and kissed his cheek complimenting how good he looked. His face immediately lit up and he smiled.

He sat at the edge of my bed holding the box tightly as if his life depended on it. Looking slightly serious for a moment, he beckoned for me to come and sit down next to him as I was standing wondering what was in the velvet black box.

"You look so beautiful, principessa – princess," I smiled warmly at him.

"Today would have been a very happy day for my son, Angelo, your papa and sure enough your dear mama, Victoria." I looked down despondently then he continued, "Even still, today is a joyous day and I know in my heart they are with us smiling down at us." He paused for a moment, "This was your mom's," he handed me the box, "She wore it on her wedding day."

I took the box from him and opened it. I was breathless; in my hands was this beautiful tiara bejeweled with a 101.27-carat shield-shaped diamond. I was near to tears but I did not want to mess up my make-up.

There was another knock at the door and it was Rosa. She was all dressed and ready. She wore a two-piece iridescent silk taffeta modified mermaid dress set, strapless ruched bodice, wrapped skirt with ruffled trim, lace jacket with ruffled taffeta trim designed by Fame Star. She looked so elegant and beautiful. I noticed she had in her hand a small red velvet box. She requested if grandpa could leave us for a moment. Once grandpa was out, she turned to me and smiled warmly.

"Victoria would be so proud of you; look at you, you look so radiant," she commented.

I gave her a hug and thanked her. I then picked up my lingerie and went to the bathroom to change. Mandy came into the room as well to help me with my dress. She too had finished dressing and looked stunning in her light gold silk strapless evening gown featuring a pleated bodice and floral-beaded empire waistband with jewels, sequins and beads embellishments. The gown was floor length with a front slit giving it an added sexiness.

She walked over to where my wedding dress was hanging; I watched with delight as she lifted my beautiful white bridal silk strapless A-line sweetheart neckline wedding gown with corset closure. I admired the style features, Swarovski crystals and delicately embellished lace adorning the bodice and center front panel insert. The crossover, asymmetrically ruched, wrapped waistline created a fabulously flattering figure that was emphasized with a corset back. Embellished lace continues along the long back train and surrounding the corset closure. I laughed as Mandy held the dress. Rosa and Mandy helped me put on the dress then Rosa presented the small velvet red box she had in her hand to me.

"Something new," she said smiling.

I took the box beaming then I opened it. Inside was a beautiful diamond earring but before I could say anything, Mandy gasped.

"Wow! That is so beautiful," she declared.

Rosa and I looked at Mandy and smiled, "Just as she said," referring to Mandy.

"Thank you, Rosa. I love it."

I put on the earrings and slipped into my Christian Louboutin shoes then I took out the diamond tiara and placed it on my head. I took a deep breath and smiled inwardly. I felt and looked like a princess; pleased with the way I looked, I turned around to face them. Rosa was speechless and was fighting back tears as well as Mandy. I walked over toward them in a slow manner and with grace. Rosa walked forward with arms stretched wide and gave me a very light hug and air kiss. I could feel the presence of my mom and dad in the room. I looked around as if I could see them.

"Joanne was so wrong when she said that you should have hired Vera Wang because celebrities tend to hire her but I think she would quickly change her mind when she sees you," said Mandy.

"Thank you, Mand," I said smiling. "We better get going, I don't want to be too late otherwise Gianni's patience might not hold," I commented. In agreement, we all went down.

My bridesmaids, flower girl and grandpa were all waiting downstairs for us. The flower girl looked so cute; she was like a miniature of me in her white dress, too; very pretty.

Oh, the weather was perfect; a radiant sunshine just nice and warm. My attention drifted to the white horses leading the white-and-gold-coated carriage waiting to carry me to the church. I could hear the girls giggling as they admired the horse and carriage before their car pulled away. Grandpa extended his right arm to escort me to the carriage. I looked at him lovingly, smiled and linked my arms with his. I squeezed his arm in appreciation. As though he understood, he looked at me smiled and patted my hand. The carriage door was opened for us, Mandy helped me with my veil then she climbed in excitedly.

A crowd lined up outside the church building waving as the horse rode by and the paparazzi busied themselves snapping here and there. When the carriage came to a stop, I was assisted in climbing down with great care. The bridesmaids and Rosa were waiting for us with the party planner. He clapped his hand for everyone to get in position as the pianist began to play. Mandy and Rosa fixed my train and veil, Rosa then handed me my white bridal bouquet then she went inside the church ahead of us. Gino came forward giving us a final look over. He came to me and pulled the veil over my face then he stepped backward, looked at me and said: "Bellissimo!"

He motioned for grandpa to take my arm and we marched forward towards the entrance of the church where everyone was waiting. I hoped Mrs. Abbott was able to make it. Once we were in view, everyone's head turned to get a glimpse of the bride. The aisle was so long it felt like forever getting to Gianni at the altar who looked as nervous as I. At long last I made it. Grandpa handed me over to Gianni and stepped aside. We faced each other gazing into each other's eyes. I knew he was overwhelmed and wanted to say so much but he did not need to speak as his eyes and expressions said it all. I could not believe we were finally there at the altar. In a matter of minutes, I would be Mrs. Canuti; wife of Gianni Canuti.

Father Severino began the service. After our vows, he asked if there was anyone who wanted to object to us becoming, husband and wife. I was confident that no one would object since my nemesis, Gina, was no longer a problem, but Gianni looked slightly unnerved, he was worried that one of my ex-boyfriends would turn up. When nobody objected, Father Severino continued and pronounced the long-awaited words.

"I now pronounce you husband and wife; you may kiss the bride."

Gianni gladly swept me up in his arms and kissed me. It was magical even though we had kissed many times but somehow this kiss was different. Everyone started clapping. We turned to face everyone with a big grin on our faces as the pianist played once again. We marched out to a waiting crowd and paparazzi snapping pictures. Confettis were thrown at us. We stood for a moment and allowed some pictures to be taken. We boarded our carriage and rode off to the first day of the beginning of our lives as husband and wife.

www.ingramcontent.com/pod-product-compliance
Lightning Source LLC
Chambersburg PA
CBHW051300170626
46809CB00004B/1734